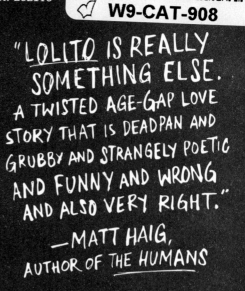
W9-CAT-908

"BOTH WARM AND UNCOMPROMISING, *LOLITO* WILL BE AS ENTERTAINING FOR YOUNG ADULTS AS IT IS EDUCATIONAL FOR OLDER READERS."
—THE GUARDIAN

"*LOLITO* IS REALLY SOMETHING ELSE. A TWISTED AGE-GAP LOVE STORY THAT IS DEADPAN AND GRUBBY AND STRANGELY POETIC AND FUNNY AND WRONG AND ALSO VERY RIGHT."
—MATT HAIG, AUTHOR OF THE HUMANS

PRAISE FOR BEN BROOKS

"The most convincing portrayal of the adolescent mind since *Vernon God Little*—Like Holden Caulfield on mephedrone." —EWAN MORRISON

"Brooks is blessed with a blinding grasp of terse, lyrical prose, and has the timing of a genius stand-up comic. Top class." —RICHARD MILWARD, author of *Apples*

"Ben Brooks is a magical imp who pumps out dark nuggets of poetry and makes you snort with laughter." —NOEL FIELDING

"It's pretty mental that Ben Brooks is any good now: imagine how good he could be by the time he actually does grow up." —*DAZED & CONFUSED*

"Brooks has an ability to show us the world through the eyes of a teenage boy and his fast-paced, expressive narration. Without all of this, we might feel as though we were being led down too many familiar paths; instead, our expectations are neatly subverted." —*SCOTSMAN*

A NOVEL

BEN BROOKS

Regan Arts.

Regan Arts.

65 Bleecker Street
New York, NY 10012

First published in Great Britain in 2013 by Canongate Books Ltd,
14 High Street, Edinburgh EH1 1TE

First Regan Arts paperback edition, July 2015.

Library of Congress Control Number: 2014955553

ISBN 978-1-941393-35-2

Typeset in Plantin by Palimpsest Book Production Ltd,
Falkirk, Stirlingshire

Cover design by Richard Ljoenes
Cover art by Clinton Reno

Printed in the United States of America

10 9 8 7 6 5 4 3 2 1

Sometimes, when one person is missing, the whole world seems depopulated.
—Alphonse de Lamartine

Fuck you, you ho, I don't want you back
—"Fuck It,"
Eamon

Prologue

We're fifteen and drinking warm cider under the cathedral grounds' pine trees. It's 7:30. There's a dim orange moon, and everything smells of just-cut grass. Alice takes out a tube of AcneGel, pushes it into my hand, and lies down, eyes closed. Sam and Aslam are talking about dogs, terrorism, and which rapper is the richest.

"Nothing above the eyebrows," Alice says. "Last time you did it above the eyebrows and it rained, and my eyes swelled up."

"But his headphones empire," Aslam says. "The headphones."

"Okay," I say.

"But some behind my ears."

"Isn't he dead?" Sam says.

"You don't have spots behind your ears."

"He's definitely alive."

"Spots might grow behind my ears."

Alice is my girlfriend. She has a sharp nose, size four feet, and Raynaud's syndrome. In the morning her mouth tastes of stale milk. I imagine her recent search history goes: *how to make a Ouija board, does anal hurt?, Haruki Murakami.*

I massage white paste onto her cheeks in small circles. She kicks off her shoes. Her feet are the shape of kites.

"I'm going away for Easter," she says. "Dad just told me. We're going on holiday. To Antigua."

"Oh," I say. I don't want her to go on holiday to Antigua. I don't know what Antigua is. For the past two years, we've spent every school break motionless in her bed, watching *CSI: New York* and eating cubes of black currant jelly.

"What's Antigua?" Aslam says.

"It's like. Um." She scrunches her nose. "No. I don't know."

"Hawaii?"

"What?"

"It's not that," I say. "It's not Hawaii."

Alice opens one eye. "You don't know what it is. You don't know about countries." I smear white down her neck and rub it into disappearance. The skin above her collarbone is thick and rough from daily benzoyl peroxide.

"I don't think it's that."

"Well, it might be." She does an *I don't want you to talk* face, pushes my hand away, and sits up. She swigs cider and diamonds appear in her cheeks, and I think again how I don't want her to go wherever Antigua is. "It definitely might be Hawaii."

"Hawaii's a country and Antigua's a different country."

"Hawaii's a state."

"I don't know what you're talking about."

"Oh," Sam says. "We're going to my aunt's in Crewe."

"You're going too?"

"Mm."

"This is retarded. What are we supposed to do?"

"I don't know."

I know what I want to do. I want to remain in bed, watching documentaries about exotic marine life and sporadically masturbating over shopping channel presenters. I want to call Alice three times a day for reassurance that she isn't putting her mouth against the mouths of people who aren't me.

"Etgar?"

"What?"

"What are you doing?"

"My parents are away. I'm not doing anything."

"Let's do something."

A wide man walks under a streetlight. He looks vaguely familiar, like I've seen him in a dream or through a car windshield. My body tenses. I imagine him holding chloroform to our faces, carrying us away, and solemnly dismembering our bodies on the floor of a urine-smelling warehouse. I press my hand against Alice's hand. "Maybe," I say.

"We could do bukkake on my dog and film it."

"I don't want to do that."

"Fine."

I watch the man shrink, disappear, then momentarily reappear under a bowl of orange light. We finish the cider and say good-bye and leave. Me and Alice go to her house. Her dad's smoking in the conservatory, so we go upstairs, turn on Radio 4, and fall asleep to unintelligible chanting.

PART 1

Titanic

1

It's the first day of the Easter holidays. Alice has gone to Antigua with her dad, and my parents have gone to Russia, to watch Uncle Michael marry a woman he found on the Internet.

I'm lying in bed.

I'm never going to move again.

I'm going to grow until I am the size of a car and the weight of a lion and my arms look like antennae. Firemen will have to cut me out of the house and a documentary crew will film it. Mum's friends will watch the documentary together, pressing their hands to their knees and mewing. *My Two Ton Son.* When I go into sudden cardiac arrest and die, they will call her to apologize and promise imminent lasagna.

Amundsen jumps onto the bed. He lies down, buries his head in my belly, and exhales. The only thing I have to do over the next four days is walk him and feed him. Mum said that if he dies, she'll put me up for adoption. She was joking but I looked it up anyway, and you can't "put people up for adoption." There's a procedure. You have to give them to Social Services.

I push Amundsen off the bed and make *go away now* eyes. He's a colossal disappointment. He drifts around dumbly, licking cushions and jumping at moths and eating his own vomit. I wanted a dog that would save my life, like Lassie, so that we could become an inseparable and inspiring team, capable of astounding feats of strength and bravery. Amundsen does nothing. If you put a blanket over his head, he instantly falls asleep.

Aslam calls while the kettle's boiling. He sounds excited and his words are melting together. He wants me to go to a house party on Huntsdon Street.

"No," I say. "Absolutely not. I'm going to make a Nesquik tea and have a bath and watch *Frozen Planet* in bed." Aslam's already called four times today, inviting me to two house parties, Shanghai Palace, and a clearing on the hill where Sam said people sometimes go to do dogging. Usually, he doesn't try to invite me to these things because I get anxious in crowded places and start to scratch my hands. When we spend time together we spend it in my bedroom or his bedroom or Alice's bedroom.

"*Frozen Planet*'s gay," Aslam says. "Stop being a pussy and come."

"It's educational, poignant, and beautifully shot. You're gay."

"Fine," he says. "Aaron Mathews is going." Aaron Mathews tried to rape Alice with kisses at a party while I was visiting Gran in Leicester. She called me at 3:00 a.m. and loudly cried for twenty-five minutes. He doesn't go to our school, and I have never seen him.

"No, he isn't," I say.

"He is. And we can fucking smash his dick in. James is coming. And Hattie."

"Are you lying?"

"I am not lying."

"If you are lying, I am going to smash *your* dick in. Also I think I am not capable of smashing dicks in, so I might just break his phone or something."

"Yeah, you can. I'll hold him down and you can crush his balls with a hammer."

"I'm not going to do that."

"Well, you should."

"Why are you going?"

"For you."

"And?"

"And also for Amy."

"I don't know who that is."

"I told you. I linked to her YouTube. She makes videos

of herself miming to rap songs. She's gone viral. I'm going to marry her."

I laugh. "I'll meet you by the sign in an hour. I'm going now. The kettle's boiled."

"Good. Bye."

I put a teaspoon of strawberry Nesquik and a teabag into my Forever Friends mug and add water. My hand is shaking slightly. I'm thinking of Alice and Aaron Mathews. I'm imagining a tall boy with impressive facial hair pressing his mouth against her neck while simultaneously squeezing her bum and left boob. I don't know if that's possible. I try it on an imaginary Alice and find that it's awkward and uncomfortable, but not impossible.

I feel small.

Like a field mouse lost in a supermarket.

Amundsen head-butts my knee and whines. He's dribbling and wagging his tail. I empty a can of tripe into his bowl and carry his bowl out onto the patio. Amundsen pushes his whole head into the bowl, motorboating his food. He lifts up his head, and blobs of tripe are clinging to his nostrils. He walks toward me and I back quickly out of the room.

I climb back into bed and turn on my computer. I meet Alice. We say hellos. She says she's having fun and that she has to go soon. I ask what they've been doing. She says they've been sunbathing and swimming. I say that sounds great. We watch a video of two men being killed. The men are members of a drug cartel. They are sitting shirtless on a dirt floor, backs against a concrete wall. The first man gets beheaded with a chainsaw. He falls onto the other man. The other man stays sitting up, and the shape of his face doesn't change, and they kill him with a bowie knife. It takes longer and involves less fireworks.

"That one was good," she says. "I've got to go. We're going out for dinner."

"Okay," I say. "I miss you."

"I miss you too."

Elliot Venn has uploaded new pictures.

Katya de Vangelo has got Joseph Gordon-Levitt, popcorn, and rosé ready for a night in with the girlies.

Carly Yates thinks that some people can just fuck off.

Horney milf wants you're cum

Sentence: ass raping til death

Dirty brit amateur swingers fuck in woods

A man and a woman are sitting side by side on thrones. They are wearing crowns and medieval clothing. The woman says that she wants King Dick to come back because her vagina is lonely. The man next to her says he is Prince Dick, and he gently presses her thigh as she bites into a turkey leg. She shouts for the archery competition to begin. Amundsen wanders back into my room, sniffs at nothing, and lies down on the rug. Three men in medieval clothing pull out their dicks and start fiercely masturbating while aiming at

a target ten feet away. I feel confused. I don't understand.

Carrie Machell is in a relationship.

I have won a free MacBook.

I take the sock off my dick and throw it at Amundsen.

2

James and Hattie are kneeling on the pavement, rubbing Clearasil into each other's cheeks. Aslam's leaning against the street sign. It's cold. He's holding a two-liter bottle of cola and a half-empty bottle of Captain Morgan's, looking at something in the sky. The blurry orange streetlight overhead lights up his face and puts his reflection in a puddle between his feet. He flaps his arms.

"Argh," I shout.

"Bah," Aslam shouts.

"Etgar," Hattie says.

"Hi."

"Hold this," Aslam says. I take the bottle of cola out of his hands and sit cross-legged on the tarmac, wedging it in the triangle of my legs. I unscrew the cap and grip it while he pours in rum. It splashes my hands. I spit and rub them on my sweater. Hattie crouches down and reaches into her bag.

"Etgar," she says. "I got you something." She passes me a lump of yellow metal.

"Thanks," I say. "What is it?"

Aslam yawns, and rum runs down my finger gaps.

"It's a knuckleduster. You put your fingers through the holes."

"Do you have Parkinson's?"

"I don't think so."

"I meant Aslam."

"Oh. Anyway, I thought you could use it on Aaron. Or wave it around in front of him until he wets himself. I remember during that carol concert when that girl wet herself doing a solo at the front in the church and you could see her trousers go dark, and then there was wee on the floor. It was amazing."

"Thanks, Hattie," I say. "That's thoughtful."

"Why do you have a knuckleduster?" Aslam says.

"It's shiny. I like it. James bought it for me. He said I was so pretty that everyone would try to rape me at sixth form." James is the only one of us who isn't going to go to sixth form in the town next door to ours. He's going to work as a plumber with his dad, who smells of orange peel and cries when football players sing the national anthem before matches. "He says I should be prepared to fight them or kill them, and he didn't want me to ruin my knuckles because they are the nicest knuckles he has ever seen."

"Gay," Aslam says. Gay doesn't mean homosexual. It means something else. It means sincerely saying the kind of things our parents would say.

"Sorry for being nice."

"Gay."

The rest of the rum disappears into the cola, and I screw on the lid and mix everything up. We pass it around.

"Have you ever hit anyone before?" Hattie asks.

"Loads," I say. "Once. No. Never. Zero times. Have you?"

"All the time. I hit Ella last week because she said I use Brillo pads for tampons, which I don't. It's easy. The secret is to pretend they're your dad."

"I like my dad."

"Someone you hate."

"I don't hate anyone."

"Then you can't really expect to be punching people."

"He has to," Aslam says, putting his hand on my shoulder and grinning. "If he doesn't, everyone will start fingering Alice." I roll a cigarette and light it, feeling unsure and insubstantial. Aslam makes a cupping motion with one hand. "Feeding his pony."

*

A girl I almost recognize opens the door of the house on Huntsdon Street. She has cropped blonde hair and is smiling and holding a bottle of Smirnoff Ice against her chest. She tells us to come inside. We come inside. People are scattered throughout the house. People are sitting and standing and talking and kissing. We drop onto an empty island of carpet next to the space heater.

"There," Aslam says, pointing at a group of three boys sitting on the stairs. "That's him. The middle one."

"How do you know?"

"Facebook."

"Is it really definitely him?" The boy is wearing stone-washed jeans and a white V-neck so low that one of his nipples is visible. There is a tribal tattoo around his forearm. "Like definitely is it that one?"

"Yeah."

"Doesn't he look a bit tall?" He looks extremely tall. The boy on his left looks like a tiger, and the boy on his right looks like an eggplant. "He has an actual tattoo."

"He's probably a fucking pussy. I'll take his knees and you take his face."

"I think we should talk to him first."

"And say what? 'Thanks for raping my girlfriend.' Fuck that. Let's smash his backdoors in." A girl to our right wrinkles her nose and raises an eyebrow. I try to smile, but my face fails to make the right shape.

"Aslam, that means butt-fucking someone."

"I thought it meant punching the back of their head."

"Why would it mean that?"

"I don't know. Just go. I've got your back."

"I'm scared."

"Just drink."

"Fine."

We take turns downing as much of the rum and coke as we can. It makes my belly pinch itself a little, but I get more brave. When we are drinking, I feel like my body becomes more solid and I am less likely to float into the sky or sink into the ground or disappear into nothing.

More people arrive, and the house shrinks. It gets loud. Someone tells James that there's nitrous upstairs, and he takes Hattie and they go.

"Ready?" Aslam asks. We've been watching two people flirt using insults by the TV.

"Yeah."

I stand up and fall to one side slightly.

"No," I say.

"Yeah," he says.

I right myself. My chest feels wobbly. I dig my fingernails into my hands until it feels like they're going to go through the skin. It takes twelve steps to reach the staircase. Twelve tiny steps. When I arrive, I panic. I stare at Aaron Mathews's shoes. They are white-and-blue Nikes. They are big. Aaron has bigger feet than anyone I know. I should make new friends. I should make new friends who have atypically large feet and intimidating physiques.

"Hi there," I say. I don't understand why I said "Hi there." I have never said "Hi there" before in my life.

"Hi there," Aaron Mathews says. He's smiling. He looks at his friends and his friends look at him, and they all do little laughs. I think about my bed and how I don't understand why I'm not in it.

"Hi there," I say again. I have no idea why I'm saying "Hi there." He should hit me. I would hit me. "Nice shoes," I say. "Very cool shoes." A reason I don't like talking to strangers is because I find it difficult to make small talk with them. Sometimes I memorize sports news for use while standing next to men at urinals, checkouts, and bus stops. Or quotes from films to fill in silences. But nothing seems relevant to now.

"Are you taking the piss?"

"No way, hoselay."

"What?"

"Um."

"Is there something you want?"

"Are you Aaron Mathews?" I ask. I look up at his face, and his face is scary, so I look back at his shoes. His nice shoes. His massive, nice shoes. I wish his face was a pair of nice shoes that I could put my feet into and jump up and down in until he apologized for what he did.

"Yes."

"Great," I say. "That's great. Do you know Alice Calloway?"

He laughs. "Yeah," he says.

"Did you rape her with kisses at all?"

"Did I what?"

"Did you force yourself on her?"

He laughs more. "Forced her off me. Little slut." He winks at one of his friends.

"Great," I say. "Thank you loads." I turn and shut my eyes as hard as I can. I want them to stitch themselves shut. I try to walk back to Aslam with my eyes still closed. Laughing happens behind me. Someone shouts at me to fuck off. I think, *Fuck off telling me to fuck off.* I think, *Where do I fuck off to?* My body is as heavy as one hundred bodies. I feel like a magician who has accidentally sawed his assistant in half. I want to disappear.

"What the fuck happened?" Aslam asks.

"He says she forced herself on him. I'm going to go."

"Fuck that," he says. "He wouldn't admit to raping her. It's not cool anymore. Go back and punch him."

"I think I'm going home."

"Fucking go back to him." He stands up and pulls me up and pushes me forward. I hold my sleeve against my eyes. I look behind me. Aslam's leaning on the mantelpiece with his arms crossed, nodding wildly. I step forward. I have no idea what I'm doing. I'm a suicide bomber. I don't believe in anything.

I walk back to the stairs and stare at Aaron Mathews and lift up my hand. It has become extremely heavy. It doesn't feel or look like my hand. Is it my hand? Probably, yes. I wonder where I should put my hand on his face. In films, people punch other people in their eyes. I don't want him to go blind, though. That would be terrible. He would sue me, and I would have to give him all of the money I got after Nan died. I should punch him in the forehead. I should say something intimidating and then knock him out.

"You better get ready," I say. "Because at 3:00 today, I'm going to rape you."

I blink.

Aaron Mathews punches me in the face.

I can't tell where exactly, but it is definitely the face. I fall over. Aslam jumps over me and lunges at Aaron Mathews. He grabs Aaron Mathews's hair. I don't think pulling hair is a very good fighting move. Jackie Chan never pulled anyone's hair. I start to stand up and the Tiger knees me in the chest. That is a good fighting move. It hurts. Fireworks explode inside my ribcage. I lie on the floor and roll to the side and look upward. The Eggplant is going through Aslam's pockets. The Tiger tries to put his hands into mine. I grab hold of his collar and throw my head against his nose. It isn't my head anymore. It isn't anything. I take Aslam's arm and pull him toward the door, and we fall through the door and run up the hill, looking backward. Nobody follows. Hard air collects inside me and burns. I imagine my legs falling off and my arms falling off and my dismembered head floating slowly up into the sky like a hot-air balloon, clouds gripping the sides of my head, flashing planes reflecting in my eyes.

We collapse onto the grass at the park and lie on our backs, panting.

When our breaths are smaller, I say, "Thanks for trying."

"Are you okay?"

"No," I say.

"You made the purple one's nose bleed."

"Oh."

"What was that rape thing from?"

"Welcome to the Dollhouse."

"You have to stop doing that."

"People say things better in films."

He leans back on his elbows and tips his head. "I think he was lying."

"I don't know."

"What will you do?"

"I don't know." I tug handfuls of grass out of the earth. In the film version of right now, I would sprint back to the house, hoist Aaron Mathews up by his Adam's apple and shake him violently until he confessed to lying. Then I would helicopter to Antigua and kiss Alice on the nose. "I'm sleepy."

3

When I was eight, Mum and I climbed onto a train, fidgeted and napped for six hours, then climbed off again in a place with sky the color of huskies and a long edge of sea. It was Scotland. Mum said that I had to stay with Nan for the summer. I was too young for clear memories of her before this one. Before this one she only existed as a collection of smells and feelings. Piss, tea, sugar. Presents, hard hugs, boredom.

"Someone's grown," Nan said, holding open the door of her cottage. I smiled. "Fat." She frowned at Mum.

"Mum," Mum said.

"Nan," I said. She pulled my face into the itchy valley between her tits. Her chest smelled of tea and old biscuits.

"Ahoy," a man said, appearing at the end of the hallway.

Nan had married a Polish man who was twenty years younger than her and wore only England rugby shirts. I was supposed to call him Uncle Sawicka. When I shook his hand, he barely squeezed, like he was scared I'd break.

"Someone looks hungry," Nan said. "Has Mummy been eating all your food?"

"Yes," I said.

"Mum," Mum said.

"Nan," I said.

Uncle Sawicka bought fish and chips, and we ate in front of the TV. Nan discussed the royal family with herself. Mum asked Uncle Sawicka about Poland. Are they pagan? Do they like chocolate? Do they have gays? I chewed my toenails until I fell asleep, balled like a fetus in the armchair. In the morning, Mum woke me up, told me to be good, and went away.

*

Nan's cottage wasn't really a cottage, it was only called that because of how it was surrounded by grass, and if you pulled the corners of your eyes upward you could kind of see the sea. There was a trailer park above it and a university across the river. I mostly stayed inside with Nan. Even when the sun visited, gray wind scared away all the warm. We pieced together jigsaws of Scottish cottages and watched *Murder, She Wrote* and drank tea that tasted different from the tea at home. Nan took me down to the sea on bright days, but she got tired quickly and we spent most of our time recovering on the rocks ("on the rocks" also meant when Nan wanted ice in her gin and tonic, which mostly she didn't. It gave her severe brain freeze).

Uncle Sawicka didn't spend a lot of time in the house. Sometimes when we met in the hallway, we'd pause and try to talk.

"Heavy weather," he'd say, looking through the glass in the front door.

"Yeah," I'd say.

"Rain," he'd say.

"Yeah," I'd say.

"Hungry," he'd say, patting my shoulder and going through to the kitchen. It's hard not to think that people who don't speak your language are morons, even when you're eight.

After two weeks, we'd established a quiet routine. Uncle Sawicka and Nan woke up early, ate together, and he left for work. I woke up at 10:00, came downstairs, and ate whatever Nan had made (scrambled eggs, toast, Corn Flakes, or hot Weetabix). Nan read and I watched TV until lunchtime, then we visited the shop or the beach, then we napped, then Scrabble, then dinner, then bed.

One day we ate without Uncle Sawicka. He was working all night posting computer parts to people who ordered them on the Internet. It was 7:00. The gray outside had gone black, and light rain was prickling the windows. Me and Nan were watching a repeat of *Bargain Hunt* on channel 409. The space heater was on and I was sitting close, even though I wasn't cold. It was never allowed to get cold in the house. If it wasn't warm enough, Nan could die.

Blue team won, the program ended, and Nan pulled herself up using only her arms.

"Nan's going to have a bath," she said. Standing in the center of the living room, hands on her hips, she looked more solid than any other human I'd met. "Give Nan a kiss." I stood up and let her smudge pink lipstick into my eyebrows. "Another half an hour and you get to bed. Do your teeth downstairs."

"Okay. Night-night."

"Good night."

She yawned, adjusted a shoulder pad, and went upstairs. I didn't want to brush my teeth. I wanted to sleep. I waited a few minutes, then followed her up and climbed into bed. Sleep wasn't hard to find. It happened. In a dream, I was being chased by an army of *Redwall* animals. Stoats, ferrets, foxes, and bears, with thin red eyes and oversized weapons. Along the River Moss, through the Mossflower woods. I could see the Abbey, but it wasn't getting closer.

They were.

They were almost here and—

I woke up with wet hair and a room devoid of angry animals. Wind was nudging the window. My mouth was dusty so I knocked back the duvet and climbed out of bed. I itched my eyes. There was still a bit of scared left in me from the dream.

"Nan?" I said. She wasn't awake. Baths make you sleepy; she taught me that. The warm makes your head slow down. "Nan?" My door was open. It was always open. I padded along the hallway, trying to keep my sound small, which was easy with the carpet being teacup-deep. The bathroom door was framed with light. Nan might have fallen asleep in the bath, I thought. Which is dangerous. You drown. "Nan?"

I pushed the door open.

Nan wasn't asleep in the bath, she was dead in it, balanced by the taps in a crumpled handstand. She was wearing green underwear and a flesh-tone bra. Her body looked bigger than usual. All the skin was piled up in one mound, sagging down over her tits and face, her gray legs pointed away from each other like TV antennae. They had the texture of kebabs.

I didn't run forward and hug her. I didn't slap her face and ask her to wake up. I didn't repeatedly say, "Please, no."

I knew Nan was dead. I'd already seen enough dead bodies on TV. This was exactly how they looked. There's no fight left under the skin, and everything flops, like a kite kept indoors. Everything goes where gravity wants because it's waiting to melt back into the ground and come back as dogs and gold and flowers. We learned about it at school. Unless you quickly put electricity into the tits, a dead person is dead.

Mum kept her voice calm when I called. She could hear the scared in mine. Talking was hard. My cheeks were thick with snot.

"Darling," she said. "Listen to me. I need you to stay calm. Go and sit downstairs. Wait for Uncle Sawicka. Please, try not to panic. Have a biscuit. I'll be there as soon as I can."

"What if. Mum. A murderer."

"Did you see someone?"

"I don't know. No. What if he's hiding? Or invisible?"

"Etgar, no one's there. Now, please, go and wait for Uncle Sawicka."

"Okay."

"Promise me?"

"Okay."

"I love you."

"Okay."

I hung up. I went into the kitchen and took two knives from the block. I turned on every light. I sat outside, to the right of the front door, down in the tall grass and the thistles, seeing bear shapes in the black.

4

I push open the door and the smell of shit climbs into my nostrils. Everything's black. I turn on the lights. Amundsen has done two shits on the living room carpet. I didn't leave the sunroom door open. I kick him. He whines. Stupid. I open the drinks cabinet and take down Dad's bottle of Famous Grouse. He only drinks whiskey during sports finals, election nights, and Christmastime, and he won't notice, and if he does, it doesn't matter. I pour some into my mouth and it hurts. I turn on the TV. It's a quiz program. A man in a blue suit is looking into the camera and rubbing his hands together like he's trying to light a tiny fire.

In which film is it said, "Some dreams come true. Some don't. Keep on dreaming"?

a) *Autumn in New York*
b) *Pretty Woman*
c) *Basic Instinct*
d) *Runaway Bride*

I shout "*B!*" at the screen. The man says he doesn't know. I call him a fucking dick idiot. I shout "*B!*" I imagine Julia Roberts aggressively hugging me until my sides go numb. Julia Roberts shampooing my hair in the bath. Julia Roberts massaging my back and purring, and reading out the Wikipedia pages of notorious serial killers to me so that I can fall gently into a deep and dreamless sleep. I pour more Famous Grouse into my mouth. The man guesses *d*. I shout "*B!*" at the screen. The answer is *b*. Alice and I watched it on a laptop while tenting under her duvet. The man is a fucking moron. The man laughs and shakes his head.

I have an idea.

I pour more Famous Grouse into my mouth.

I go upstairs and turn on my computer. I play Salem.

Kayleigh Evans just had a wicked night with Mary, Sarah, and Chris at Liquid.

Miles Drinkwater passed his driving test today.

Dannie Everton is now employed by the Queen's Arms.

Alice has used my computer to log into her Facebook. This means that her password might have been saved by autofill. This means I can get into her Facebook. This means I can find out if Aaron Mathews was lying.

I get into her Facebook.

Chris Parsons is looking forward to his London trip tomorrow. Time for bed.

Dear Chris Parsons, fuck you. Nobody cares.

Alice's profile picture is of her and her dad on the beach in Antigua. I think, *Where the fuck even is Antigua?* I think, *Fuck you.* Marie Denton is online. Marie Denton is Alice's best friend. Marie Denton is grade seven on the clarinet and was briefly addicted to diazepam.

"Hi," I say. "Antigua is fun. I am having an amazing time here haha." This is an accurate impersonation of Alice. She types that she's laughing even when she is definitely not laughing.

"Hi," Marie says. "Cool. You have Internet?"

"Just for a minute. I needed to ask you something."

"Are you okay?"

"Yes. Just I've been feeling bad about the Aaron Mathews thing. I'm not sure if I should tell Etgar the truth."

"Why?" she says. "You didn't even properly fuck him and you were drunk."

The feeling that happens in my head is the same as when you wake up after sleeping on an arm. A warm, staticy lack of feeling. I'm still for a little, then I'm not. The blood comes back.

I think, *Fucking fuck shit fuck.*

I think, *Am I going to vomit?*

I'm maybe going to vomit.

I throw my computer off the bed. I'm shaking. My heart is beating fast and my chest feels tight. I think, *Am I going to have a heart attack?* I hope I don't die of a heart attack. If that happens someone will say something retarded about me dying "from a broken heart."

I go into the bathroom and take the Tylenol Mum was given for her gout out of the cabinet. Downstairs, I break ten of the tablets in half and put them into a cup. My hands are shaking and everything is hard to do. Everything is heavy and slow. I add water and crush everything with the handle of a screwdriver. I take off my trousers and my boxer shorts and stretch the boxer shorts over a pint glass and pour the mixture through. A pyramid of white powder collects on top of the boxer shorts. Acetaminophen. I throw it away. I drink the mixture. I hold my own hands to try and stop them from shaking, and my whole body starts to shake and I think I'm going to fall over. I go upstairs and lie on top of my duvet. Amundsen lies next to me. I push my face into his fur. A low moaning sound comes out of me and he does a little grunt. I think to myself, *See you in the morning.*

5

I wake up and sit up and shake my head. There are tiger cubs inside of it. Last night's dream is still hanging around my eyes. Something about a bear and a basement. And Drake. Or Paul Rudd. A river. I don't remember. For a second, nothing happens. My head is a tomb. And it's one of the best feelings, next to paying with exact change and narrowly escaping rain. When you wake up and the people in your head sit still.

Then it starts.

Everything hurts.

I want to vomit.

I imagine never moving. I imagine a camera filming my body as it decomposes and the footage being sped up so that it looks like I'm being eaten by the air. Alice.

Alice and Aaron Mathews. Aaron Mathews's hand inside Alice. Aaron Mathews's dick inside Alice's mouth.

Amundsen's moved and is asleep at the bottom of my bed. His whole body is expanding and contracting like a slowly beating heart. It's raining. It's raining a lot. I push the duvet away and Amundsen flounders, appears momentarily confused, then gets to his feet and jumps onto the carpet. We stand at the window. I groan. I press my nose against the glass. Someone is hurling buckets of water against it, over and over. Amundsen licks my hand. I scratch behind his ear.

I'm dizzy.

I shiver.

I go into the bathroom and run my face under the cold tap.

"Up," I say. "Breakfast." Amundsen follows me downstairs and waits next to the kettle as it boils. Nesquik tea can upset my stomach, so I have normal tea. Amundsen has tripe. I try to eat a Ryvita cracker, but it's too dry, forming small bricks in my cheeks that refuse to shift. I eat cherry yogurt. My phone rings and I have to answer. It's Mum.

"Etgar?" she says. "Etgar, it's Mum."

"I know. I'm here."

"Are you okay? Is everything fine? Is Amundsen alive?" I look at Amundsen. Drops of water and saliva are hanging from his muzzle like icicles from a rooftop.

"He's alive," I say. "Everything's fine."

"Are you eating okay? Did we leave enough?"

"Everything's fine. How's Russia?"

"Oh, it's wonderful. Your Uncle Michael is very happy, and Alena is lovely."

"Have they done it yet?"

"Done what?"

"The marrying."

"The ceremony's tomorrow. It's going to be in this gorgeous little church surrounded by beautiful fields."

"Great. That sounds great."

"I'd better go. This is expensive, and we've got to go shopping for a present. Are you sure you're okay?"

"I'm okay. Say hi to Dad. You should buy them a dog for when she runs away."

"Etgar, be nice."

"Sorry. Bye, Mum."

"I love you."

"You too."

I sit on the sofa and feel like I'm the *Titanic*. Amundsen gets up next to me and puts his head in my lap. He dribbles onto my leg, and saliva soaks through my trousers. I try to play At Least. Here:

– At least I'm not dead (How good is this? Maybe being dead is good. Maybe all of the religions are real and when you die you go somewhere fun and infinite).

– At least I'm not old (I'm older than yesterday).

– At least I don't have cancer (I might have cancer. I cough all the time).

– At least I don't have to do anything (I have to walk Amundsen).

I don't remember all of last night. There are gaps. I remember Marie. I remember Aaron. My phone's flashing. One new message.

Alice to me: *What? U drnk? Miss you txt mexx.*

I check my sent messages.

Me to Alice: *fjkyyyyyyyuuuuuuuuuuuuu.*

Upstairs, I pick up my laptop. The plastic casing has come open and circuit boards are peeking out. It's blank. Last night it showed a tiny nightmare. I don't know what I want it to show anymore. I scratch my balls. I want it to show naked women who aren't Alice.

I go to get Mum's laptop. She won't know, as long as I delete everything. I close my bedroom door and climb into bed and pull the duvet over my head. Amundsen paws at the door. I decide to find out if chatrooms still exist. Adult sex ones. The ones I used to play on in computer lab at school when there was nothing else to do. Ones filled with people bored of work and of sitting at home and of being alone. Where people don't really say anything, they just type because what else.

They still exist.

There's one called chatworld.

There's one called adultchatlife.

There's one called battychat.

Battychat doesn't sound like something I would be interested in. I click on adultchatlife and select the "adult chat" category. Lines of words and emoticons and laughter flash and scroll up as quickly as numbers in a matrix. If people laughed and smiled that often in real life then real life would be markedly more bearable. If the whole of real life was one big chatroom, then everyone would have to be honest with everyone else and no one would secretly sort of fuck Aaron Mathews and no one would be alone. I think, *Don't think about that.* I give myself the name Herman441.

Missyeti: lol @ Sammy

Overandouty: frog = Corinne

Stud40: frog would be too small

Corin19: fuck off over

Macy1: lol cor

Sweetballs: anyone ever fuked a animal

Biggybigbig: lol

Homealone002: lol

Mistymale: haha

I don't understand. I scroll up and there's a link to a video. I click. The video is of a chimp sitting on a flat, dirty island of straw in its zoo enclosure. It's holding a frog in its hands and raping the frog's mouth. Me and

Alice watched this video two years ago. It was Alice's fourth-favorite, after *Zombie Prank*, *Haunted Toaster*, and *24-Hour Nyan Cat*.

Entropy: how u make dog suck ur dick
Sweetballs: put sugar on
77ACE77: this vid is sick

I try to think of a joke that will endear me to the group. A simple, bad joke that will make a woman think I'm the kind of person worth pressing her tits against a camera for.

Herman441: froggy style
Stud40: lol
Corin19: haha
Macy1: hahahahahaha
Missyeti: skullfuck
Macy1: I am laughing

I type more things, and other people type more things. We talk about sexual positions and types of porn and types of tea and how to record audio from YouTube videos. We are bored people with nowhere to be and nothing to do. It is fun, and it means I don't have to think. I play Gold Panda in the background to make myself go calm. Alice sends me a text, and I turn off my phone.

Macy1: Herman I'm pming you my gmail
Tinybearo: does anyone got legit zooey deschanel nudes is that exist
Stud40: macy add me I'm chachaman@yahoo.com
Herman441: okay

Macy1 to Herman441: my gmail is macyishiding@ gmail.com add me so we can chat properly. I think you're funny.

Herman441 to Macy1: You're nice too. I'm at work right now and I have some stuff to do. I'll add you when I get home so we can chat. Hi.

Amundsen's still pawing at the door, so I open it and let him in. He bounds in circles around the room, comes to a stop, and tries to make me stroke him by assaulting my hand with his face. He wants to go for a walk. The rain has almost stopped. There are only tiny flecks of water settling on my window now. Leaving the house is scary. I'm worried the sky will get too heavy and I'll fall over. I think about Aaron Mathews pumping his hand backward and forward inside of Alice's vag. I think about Alice's mouth being open as wide as a mouth can be open, so wide that it cracks and splits at the corners. I think about her asking him to choke her.

I should go for a walk.

People like walks.

I don't like walks.

We go downstairs and I attach Amundsen's lead. I put on Mum's purple raincoat, Dad's bucket hat, and my old wellies. I look like a pedophile.

6

The field opposite our house is a collection of rugby pitches surrounded by lanky, coniferous bushes. There's an oak tree in one corner where boys with bicycles sit to smoke weed and punch each other in the head. Mostly people walk their dogs in laps around the edge. When it snows, this is where everyone comes. When it snows, this is the battlefield, but today it's almost empty.

I let Amundsen off the lead, and he immediately runs to a Coke can, sniffs it, and shits on it. He looks back at me and wags his tail and grins. I tell him he's done a great job. The only other person in the field is a tall man in a felt coat walking an orange terrier on a lead. The terrier keeps running ahead and the man doesn't, so it gets pulled up on its back legs like a drawbridge.

We walk slowly.

The sky is pink and the moon is a ghost. Amundsen examines condoms and plastic bags while I think about Alice. I try not to think about Alice, which means that I am thinking about Alice. I think about jumping off a tall building and leaving a note behind that says "Alice Calloway murdered me." I probably shouldn't do that. I definitely won't do that. If I did that, then I would be dead and Alice would be upset, so it is a lose/lose. Do I want Alice to be unhappy? I don't want Alice to be unhappy. I want Alice to go back in time and be unfingered by Aaron Mathews.

The wind hums.

It starts to rain. It crescendos. We're halfway around the field. I don't want to run. I'll fall over if I try. I'll fall over and I won't want to stand up and I'll lie in the grass and sad dogs will eat my body. Maybe I should do that. It might be fun. I clip on Amundsen's lead, and we climb in between two of the bushes and sit on a muddy bank behind them, facing the back of a black garden fence. The rain gathers pace and tumbles down louder. It makes the ground hiss and the air smell like wet soil. Drops of water drip from the ends of branches. I shiver. I press my nose against Amundsen's nose. I feel like I'm going to fall into the ground.

"Room at the inn?" I look to my left. A miniature woman in a yellow raincoat has appeared. She's holding a small dog. Wet, white curls of hair are stuck down against her forehead. Her face is dappled like bruised banana skin.

"Um."

"This is cosy," the woman says. She pushes the bushes aside and climbs in and sits down. "You did good. Cats and dogs. It'll be fish next. You wait." She smiles at Amundsen and strokes him with both hands. "Who do we have here?"

"Amundsen."

"Amundsen, that's a name. Who gave him that?"

"I did," I say. "After Roald Amundsen. The first man to reach the South Pole. He got hungry and ate his dogs."

"Big shoes. I'm sure you'll manage. Won't you? This one's called Mushroom. After mushrooms. Love them. Absolutely love them." I laugh. Mushroom climbs over Amundsen and arranges himself in my lap. He's the size of a shoebox. "He likes you."

"Oh."

"I'm Mabel."

"Etgar." We shake hands. Mabel's palm feels like car tires.

"You're at school?"

"St Catherine's."

"Good. That's a good place. How old does that make you?"

"Fifteen."

"You're a big fifteen. Look at those bones. Sports bones they are. Rugby bones. I'm seventy-two. Do you know, a man on the radio yesterday said we're all going to live to be two hundred. Two hundred. Imagine that."

"That would be terrible."

"Dear lord. I'd rather jump off a bridge. Two hundred years. Two hundred years. What would you do with two hundred years?"

"TV."

"Oh God, and wouldn't you? They'd put a 100–200 category into *X-Factor*. Each episode would last four hours."

I laugh again.

"No school today?"

"Easter holidays."

"Ah. Easter. Eggs.'"

"My parents are away in Russia. I'm alone."

"Alone," she says. "Then it's good we've both got these strong young men to look after us." She nods at the dogs. I look down at Mushroom. He's licking my knee. We sit, not saying anything, until the rain gets quieter and slower. Mabel tells me that she walks Mushroom at the same time every day, so maybe we'll see each other tomorrow. I say that I would like that. The dogs shake themselves off and we climb out of the bushes.

*

I'm sitting at the kitchen table. Amundsen's lying on my

feet. I can feel his heartbeat through my toes. He's asleep and making sounds like a big man shivering. I'm drinking Nesquik tea and eating microwave lasagna and watching a video of a man putting a kitten into a wire cage then setting it on fire. I don't know why. It's boring.

I click on Alice Calloway. I open her photo albums.

Berlin 09: Alice wearing the red dress with miniature horses on it. Alice holding a coffee mug the size of a baby. Alice outside the Reichstag, pretending that an inflatable hammer is her dick.

Snow day 10: Me sitting on Alice's chest in a field of snow. Alice with a snowball in her mouth. Aslam punching Sam. Sam punching Aslam. Alice bagging Aslam's trousers.

I should stop doing this. It isn't fun and it isn't helping.

Geography trip Lulworth: Alice straddling an orange rock. Alice hugging Emma. Alice building sandcastles. Georgie drawing a dick in the sand.

I don't want to do this anymore.

Sarah's 18th: Alice and Sarah and Emma and Paige standing by a row of black shots lined up on a bar. Alice with both of her arms in the air. Alice and a topless man through a fisheye lens. Emma puking at a bus stop.

I don't understand why I'm doing this. I feel sick.

Georgie's: Alice on a horse, holding a bottle of Smirnoff Ice. Emma giving Alice a love bite. Georgie's mum downing shots. Alice hugging Georgie's mum. A close-up of Alice's face, grinning wildly through smudged orange lipstick.

I slam the computer shut and punch it. I'm crying. If I was the subject of a documentary, then this would be the part where I smash the camera and hit the cameraman. I would shout, "Get that fucking camera out of my face, it's over."

My phone flashes.

Hattie to me: *u okay? Aslam told me.*

Me to Hattie: *I'm just going to hide a while. I'm okay.*

Hattie comes over sometimes and we touch each other because we're bored and because what else. I don't know what now. I should stop looking at Alice. I rub my eyes with my T-shirt and open a bottle of Mum's Merlot and fill a pint glass with it. I add Macy on gchat. She's online. She says hi.

"Hi," I say.

"Work over?"

"Yes."

"Where are you?"

"UK. You?"

"Same."

I blink. She's closer than I expected. I always think of people in computers as existing in a quiet, distinct place that almost never overlaps with real life. "Where?" An unpronounceable, politically stable country with national service and bidets.

"Inverness."

I search Inverness. It's in Scotland. There are pictures of green hills and thick clouds and wide, metallic bodies of water. "Oh," I say. "The prosperous hub of the Highlands." That sounds too formal. "Old Invy." Good one. She's going to disappear.

"Haha."

"What do you do there?"

"Look after my kids. Housework. Nothing exciting."

"Great," I say. That's a stupid thing to say. "I mean it must be nice to have free time."

"I guess," she says. "But it can get lonely around the house."

"You don't have a husband?"

"Would I be in chatrooms if I did?"

"I don't know."

"Not many men are interested in a woman with two kids. And there's only so much you can do on your own."

"Like what."

"Haha you know like what."

"No I don't."

"You're funny. What do you do, hon?"

I think of a job and search it.

"I'm a mortgage broker," I say. "I act as an intermediary who brokers mortgage loans on behalf of individuals or businesses." I think, *Is that convincing?* I think, *Maybe not.* Still too formal. She's a woman, not a boardroom. I decide to add a personal touch to make it convincing. "Mainly for individuals," I say. "Mainly for women."

"Oh," she says. "High-powered."

Nothing happens. I fill up the kettle and put it on. I try to fit my fist inside my mouth.

"I haven't seen you around the rooms before," she says.

"It was my first time."

"It's hard to find anyone sane."

"The people seemed weird. That man who kept typing about sex with animals."

"It's mostly people like that. Every now and again you meet someone worth talking to. Is Herman your real name, hon?'"

I have no idea what "hon" is.

Is anyone's real name Herman?

"No. It's Etgar."

"Mine's Macy."

"Hi Macy."

"Hi."

"What do you normally do in rooms?'"

"Not much. I have a few friends that I like to mess about with. Like Corinne. Just meet people really. Chat. Anything. Sometimes other stuff."

"What other stuff?"

"Haha. Like cyber and stuff."

"Oh."

"You ever cyber?"

"Yes," I say. "Loads."

Literally never.

"I prefer real life . . . but sometimes it's not possible."

"What do you look like?"

"Pic for pic?"

"Okay. Wait. I'll take one."

I go upstairs and open Dad's wardrobe. There are shirts of various colors on hangers with ties threaded through them. A black one looks small. I put it on without a tie and button it up to the top. I unbutton four buttons. I button up two buttons. I push my hair back. It looks like Bugsy Malone.

On the computer screen my face looks tiny and new. If I turn my head slightly to one side and tip it back then my jaw looks more like the jaw of a mortgage broker. I need to make her want me. I need to be six Aaron Mathews.

"You took one?" Macy asks.

"Almost."

Alice to me: *I miss you txt meeeeeeeeexxxxxxxxxx.*

I make the photo black and white. I make it sepia. I chug some wine. I make it black and white again.

"I did one," I say. "I look stupid."

"Send it. I sent mine."

I open the email and download the attachment. The woman who appears in my computer is thin and blonde and attractive. She looks strong, like someone who could punch through walls. I would guess that she is thirty-five, but I can't really tell because I'm not good with ages greater than my own. Her skin is the color of buttered toast. She is smiling and her teeth sit together perfectly like bathroom tiles. I don't know why she is looking for sex on computers. She should be having passionate, physical sex with men who trim their pubic hair and compete, successfully, in triathlons.

"You're beautiful," I say. "Amazing eyes."

Amazing nipples showing through the T-shirt.

"That's sweet. Your turn."

"I'm scared. I look really stupid. You're the winner."

"Send it."

"Okay."

I send it and I wait.

"You're handsome. Relax. You have good eyes. I like your shirt."

"Thanks," I say. "It's mine."

"You're funny."

"Thanks." I don't know what to say. "What will you do today?"

"Do laundry. Wash dishes. Try to forget I'm doing either. Nothing exciting. You?"

"Maybe watch television and go to bed. Nothing exciting either." Amundsen comes out from under the table and pushes his face into my leg.

"Tell me what it's like where you are. I want to try and picture it."

I look around the kitchen. There are four plates, two mugs, and a dirty French press stacked next to the sink. All of the surfaces are black, and the floor is cheap laminate. The pint glass next to me is half-full.

"I'm in my study," I say. "I'm sitting in an extremely luxurious swivel chair. The carpet is deep and red. If I put my bare feet on it my toes disappear. There are Daniel Clowes prints on the walls." Amundsen head-butts my knee.

"Sounds perfect."

"What's it like where you are?"

"Well, I'm lying on my bed. It's king-size and it always feels empty. My carpet is green. There are two big windows. You can see woods and a part of the loch. It's bright outside, and there aren't any clouds."

"I wish I could climb into yours."

"No, you don't."

"Why not?"

"It's no fun if you can't climb back out again." I don't know what she means. I still want to climb into it. I want to be anywhere that isn't here. Amundsen rears up and drops his paws onto my thigh. He wants to go outside, and I want him not to shit in the house.

"I have to go," I say. "I'm sorry."

"It was fun talking. Let's do it again."

"Okay."

I close the computer and go into the sun room and open the patio doors. We stand and look out at the garden.

Sideways rain hits my nose and forehead. Amundsen steps back.

"Please go outside," I say. "If you shit in the house I'm going to make you eat it." He looks up at me and his eyes wobble. "Come on," I say. "It's only rain. You're a brave dog."

Still nothing. I sigh. I stand behind him and reach underneath his belly and lift him. He screams and thrashes in my arms like a massive fish. I lose my balance, reach out at invisible hands, and fall onto the patio. I lie on the wet paving stones and rain beats down on my back. I don't ever want to move. I want to be abducted by calm, quiet aliens who are searching distant planets for docile zoo exhibits. Amundsen slowly walks out, lowers his face to mine, and licks my eye.

Alice Poem #1
You are shit and your birthmark looks
like a fat monkey not like a dandelion I said that
because I like sexing you. In bed you
are like an uncooked joint of beef. Your
birthmark is a giant walrus. Your birthmark
is a dead walrus crying black tears into the
Gulf of Mexico oil spill. You are BP and we
are the Macondo Prospect. Today the bath
felt as big as one hundred baths. I missed
you today. You are shit, idiot.

7

When I'm in bed, Aslam calls and tells me to come to the Bricklayer's Arms. I tell him I don't want to, that I've lost my fake ID, so I'm going to stay in bed, watch *Parks and Recreation,* and drink this disgusting wine. He says he knew I'd say that and he's made me a breakup plan.

1. Call her and tell her to go and eat a bag of dicks. Also break up with her.
2. Have sex with a prostitute in the £50–70 price bracket. ("Can you get them for that?" "Yes, I checked." "Okay, I'm not going to." "You should, man." "No.")
3. Have sex with a girl who isn't a prostitute. ("Why did you need to put the prostitute bit in?" "For

practice." "It's disgusting." "Loads of people do it." "Who?" "Every single rapper in the world." "Not Will Smith." "Probably Will Smith.")

4. Cocaine. ("Aslam, when have we ever done cocaine?" "That time in the woods by Matt's." "That was like speed and mephedrone. It might have even been crushed-up sweeteners." "How do you know?" "I kissed Sarah and Ben didn't sleep for two days. But he drank four Red Bulls too, so I don't know." "Okay, fine. Do some drugs, though." "I'm not going to do drugs on my own. I ate some of Mum's Tylenol." "Okay, cross this one off.")

5. Go to the pub with Aslam.

"I'm not coming out," I say. "Alice sort of sexed Aaron Mathews. Nothing is ever going to happen ever again. I'm staying in bed."

"You have to get back on the wagon sometime."

"That means not drinking."

"Does it?"

"Yes. What's wrong with you?"

"Come out."

"No."

"I'm going to do an intervention on you."

"I'm not letting you into my house. I'll lock everything." Me and Aslam sometimes play a game where we break into each other's houses. You have to find a way in and sneak up on the other person and shout "Police!"

"You're being a dick," Aslam says.

"I want to not do anything."

"I'm trying to help."

He hangs up. I don't understand why people can't just let other people lie in their beds and slowly disappear if that's what they want to do. People are allowed to get facial tattoos and sex changes and speedboats, but I'm not allowed to stay in bed for four days. Aslam's being a dick. Amundsen nudges the door open and climbs up next to me. He never makes me go to the Outside and sit in pubs and talk about girls with him. He's a perfect friend.

*

Amundsen wakes me up with ear licking. Morning colors wiggle under my eyes. I stare at the ceiling. I imagine Damien Hirst pulling the roof off and pouring formaldehyde into my bedroom. Me and Amundsen will never move again. We'll sit in the middle of a museum until someone buys us for one million pounds.

It's still raining.

I go downstairs and boil the kettle and make Nesquik tea. Amundsen goes into the garden to touch things with his nose. He plays staring with a squirrel near the dead apple tree. I look at the mound where the butter knife is buried and feel somehow like I miss my eleven-year-old self. I imagine sitting with him on the sofa, simultaneously scratching our hands and talking about how everything outside of this house is upsetting and unnecessary.

I make a cigarette. My phone shakes.

Alice to me: *wer r u? I want to come home now. Let's watch evry Wes Anderson in my bed.*

There's a bald man on the television saying that another man has died. Ariana Grande comes on and a blonde woman asks her questions about nothing. Ariana Grande smiles and looks at a camera and says something about being yourself. I don't want to be myself, Ariana. Leave me alone. The bald man appears again. The bald man says things about money and debt. None of it is real. None of it is happening. The only real thing is Alice. Alice is the only thing that exists. Alice doesn't exist anymore. Alice and Aaron Mathews. They are still sort of having sex in my head. He is extremely well-endowed. Big feet. The bald man points at me. He knows everything.

"Following the emergence of leaked information regarding Alice Calloway, Etgar Allison has suffered considerable loss of motivation, energy, and interest in his usual pursuits (Wikipedia, YouTube, Kurt Vonnegut). He has been seen to spend long periods of time staring at inanimate objects and will occasionally stop whatever he is doing to lie facedown on the floor and sing 'A

Thousand Miles' by Vanessa Carlton (a song he has described as 'all that's left').

"In an official statement given earlier today, he described bed as 'better than sex' and Alice Calloway as 'the horriblest bitch I know.'"

I go back up to my bedroom and sit in the middle of my carpet with Mum's computer. Macy's online.

"Hi," she says.

"Hi."

"Are you at work?"

"Yes."

"What can you see?"

I look at the bonsai tree Mum bought me for Christmas. Its leaves are composting in piles along my windowsill. The sky behind is gray and empty.

"The whole of London. It's raining a little. There are red lights on the tops of buildings. The sky is pink and orange."

"Sounds beautiful."

"It is but there are people next to it, and things with people next to them aren't fun." That sounds too bleak. Stop being bleak. "I mean too many people. There are a lot of people, and I don't want to see them."

"At least you get to meet girls if you want to."

"You don't get to meet men?"

"Sometimes, when my ex takes the kids. Usually there's no time."

"So you cyber?"

"Sometimes."

"I don't really go out and meet girls."

"Why not?"

Because they tend not to go for fifteen-year-old boys with back acne and anxiety issues.

"Because I'm not very good at it."

"You're fine at it," she says. "And you're young. You probably pick them up in clubs by sliding drinks down bars and winking."

"I don't do that," I say. "I don't slide glasses at people. I'd worry about the glass smashing and pieces going on the girl and her suing me."

"A man did it to me once and I slid the drink back to him."

"I'd be scared of that."

"But it's nice to have drinks slid at you."

"I guess."

"Yes."

"What are you doing now?"

"Just chatting. Kids in bed."

"I still wish people could climb through computers."

"Me too. Just not to here. You should try."

"I'm trying. My face is against the screen. It isn't working. Maybe there's like something you need to press. Like F5 or something."

"Haha. Do you have cam?"

"It's broken, sorry." It's not. I have one. I don't want

her to realize I'm a boy. I want to see her. "You could put yours on."

"Not if you don't. I'm not a cinema."

Nothing happens.

"What would happen if you could climb through the computer?" Macy asks.

"I don't know. I'd appear in your bedroom. Would you be scared?"

"No. You're not scary."

"I'm scary."

"Haha."

"I've killed people with my hands. I'm wanted in several exotic countries, and there is a fatwa on my head."

"For?"

"Stealing yachts and liberating circus animals."

"Did anyone die?"

"Not this time."

"Okay."

"I think I'd stare at you for a while. If I appeared."

"I feel sort of horny imagining you appearing."

"Oh."

"Stop staring and come over here."

"Wait. What are you wearing?"

"Jeans and a black lace bra."

"You look nice."

"What are you wearing?"

"A suit."

"Are you going to kiss me?"

"Okay. Sorry. I'm doing it. Kissing."

"It's nice when you do that."

I don't understand.

"I've moved to your neck. It's warm."

"I'm pulling your hair."

"Stop pulling my hair and take off your trousers."

I put on Crystal Castles. I feel aggressive and sexual. I don't know who I am.

"Open yours under the desk and hold your cock."

"Okay."

I take off one of my socks and pull it over my dick. I stare at the computer.

"Are you hard?"

"Yes."

"Good. I'm wet."

"I'm sitting on the floor. I'm lightly kissing your ankles."

"Go on."

"Slowly moving up your calves. Dragging my tongue over your skin." Is "dragging my tongue" sexy? It doesn't seem very sexy.

"My legs are on your shoulders. You're kissing my thighs."

"I'm running my tongue over them. I'm kissing your pants." I should stop putting my tongue on stuff. I sound like a dog.

"Hold on, hon. I'm getting a vibe."

This isn't real. Things like this don't happen. Macy's

a robot. My dick is massive. I want to fall through the computer and into her. I want everything to disappear.

"I'm here. You've made me wet."

"Great. That's really good."

"Can you feel my wet with your tongue?"

"Yes. You taste nice."

I am a terrible and disgusting human being.

"Push my panties to the side."

"Don't tell me what to do, you stupid bitch."

Truly repulsive and pathetic.

"I'm not into that."

"Okay, sorry." This isn't like on TV at all. "I've pushed them aside. I'm tickling your pussy with my tongue." Do people actually like hearing this? This is the easiest way of making people happy ever invented.

"Keep going."

"You're so wet. A lake."

"Mm. Are you touching yourself?"

"Yes."

"In the office. That's so hot. I've turned my vibe up to max."

An actual, real dildo.

Unbelievable.

"My hand is moving quickly." Too boring. "Like I'm firing celebratory shots into the air." Too much.

"Come up."

"Okay."

"Kiss me."

"I am."

"I can taste myself. Now push me over your desk."

"Okay. I'm pushing your face against it and pulling your pants down to your ankles."

"Fuck me."

"I am."

Who am I? I'm not me anymore. I don't say these things. I've been possessed by a gross and lonely ghost.

"Fuck."

"Fuck."

"Oh God."

I cum. I pull the sock off my dick and throw it against a wall.

"Shit," I say. "Someone's knocking on my door. I need to go. This was fun."

"Fuck. Fuck, hon. That was great."

I stare at my feet. I watch a video of a severely disabled person covering a Katy Perry song. I run a bath.

8

When I was small I thought of the Outside as a large bear populated by an infinite amount of miniature bears. Bears that wanted to throw me over their shoulders, carry me away, and perform strange sexual acts on me until they were ready to beat my broken body to death with crowbars and pickax handles. Morticians would be paid to reconstruct my figure. Mum would fail to recognize me.

This sounds dramatic.

I was a dramatic little human.

I came back from Scotland and spent most evenings alone in my room, watching documentaries about African wildlife and reading books about places that didn't exist. Sometimes I dreamed about Nan as a zombie, wanting to pin me down and tear clumps of wet meat from my chest. When summer arrived, Mum made me go into the Outside. I went to Ben Wheelan's, who was the only person I interacted with at school through our shared appreciation of raisins, kicking rocks, and not being in classrooms. We played PlayStation and dammed the brook in the park with rocks and Coke cans. Ben Wheelan once dared himself to eat a whole chili pepper, then threw up on my shoes. His hobbies included: Good Charlotte, yo-yos, and wiping his dick on stuff before giving it to people. He showed me how to gel my hair like Ross from *Friends,* and he taught me that if you think of it as one, toothpaste becomes a tasty midnight snack.

Age ten, I walked home from his house on a hot day over the holidays. Everywhere was deserted. Streetlights were turning themselves on. The silhouettes of trees punched black octopuses out of the sky. I dropped my scooter and crouched down to try and make conversation with a tired-looking cat. I had read that they were capable of this. This cat wasn't. It licked itself and said nothing.

The cat left. A car pulled up next to me. My body jammed. Its door opened. Someone stepped out and stepped forward and said to come over.

I ran.

The person followed quickly behind me. Their footsteps made heavy echoes like someone clapping in an empty hall. I dragged my scooter along, getting dizzy and dizzier still. My heart panicked and yelped and my legs caught fire and I eventually collapsed in the hallway of our house, unraped and unmurdered.

The next day I asked Ben Wheelan, "If someone is chasing you, is it faster to run or go on your scooter?"

"Smack their head with your scooter," he said.

At home, in the garage, I picked my scooter up by the handlebars and tried to swing the standing-on part at an invisible bear. It swung all the way around and into the back of my head. When I woke up, there was a lump that felt like an extra head throbbing on the back of mine. It made me think of Voldemort's head being on the back of Professor Quirrell's. I went inside and made a pint of strawberry Nesquik and cried. I took a butter knife from the cutlery drawer and buried it at the bottom of my school bag. The first weapon.

9

My body is tired and my head is tired and everything inside of my head is tired. I listen to Vanessa Carlton and jump on the bed. It makes *I am ready to fall apart* sounds. I think about actually walking one thousand miles, nonstop, toward a secret castle lined with blankets and wildlife posters. I think about sitting in bed with Vanessa Carlton and exchanging love bites and crying into her hair. It hurts, Vanessa. Really lots. A head-butt to the heart. Make it stop. Make it disappear. Let's hide inside each other. Let's never go outside.

The doorbell rings.

I'm scared to answer the door but I do, in case it's someone from a television prank show coming to tell me that it's all a big joke. A joke that Alice and Marie and Aaron Mathews are all in on. They will have put tiny cameras in every corner of my house. *My Pathetic Boyfriend.* When Ashton Kutcher reveals the truth, I will try to laugh, but I will be crying heavily.

It's not Ashton Kutcher. It's Hattie.

She's wearing a yellow dress and a parka and large, metal earrings. She's holding two Tesco bags and a blue duffel bag.

"Hattie," I say. "You're at my house."

"Aslam said you might need cheering up," she says, pushing past me. "I am here to do that. I brought oven chips and chicken strips and *Titanic*. Also, you can borrow my panda suit."

"Thanks," I say. I stare at a man talking on his phone in the street. I close the front door.

"Here. Put it on." She passes me the duffel bag.

"Now?"

"It'll make you feel better."

"Will it?"

"Put it on. I'll put the food in."

"Thanks."

"Go on."

Me and Hattie never have sex. We dry-hump each other and kiss. She gave me a handjob once, but it hurt and I told her to stop. It's fun. It never matters that James and Alice exist, because we aren't doing anything wrong, because nobody gets upset. Alice did it wrong. I can tell because I'm upset. She could have sexed one hundred people and if I hadn't found out, she wouldn't have done anything wrong. People say lots of nice things about honesty, and I think that honesty is like a piñata with nothing inside. People should make other people happy, and you don't need to be honest to do that.

I wish *Eternal Sunshine of the Spotless Mind* was real. As Jim Carrey, I would be extremely happy to let Kate Winslet disappear from inside of my head. I wouldn't fight. I wouldn't run around in memories trying to stop her evaporating. I would say good-bye and kiss her and forget about her forever. That is probably the only way ever to be happy.

Keep saying bye.

I should hit myself with something heavy and give myself amnesia.

Joking.

I reappear in the panda suit. It's oversize and extremely comfortable. I'm a safe toddler. We go upstairs and lie on the bed and put *Titanic* in. Hattie watches *Titanic* once every three days. She says it gives her good perspective.

We lie on our backs and Hattie puts her hand on my hand.

"How many times did you see it this week?" I say.

"I watched it once already. I was going to watch it yesterday, but there were too many moths in my room. They come when I'm menstruating. Mum says it's the smell."

"Oh."

"Do you want to talk about Alice? It's okay if you do. I never even liked her that much really, because she thinks that ghosts are real, which they aren't. Also I don't think she should have instagrammed her mum's grave so much."

"Me neither."

"Do you want to take it in turns saying things we don't like about her?"

"Um."

"She smells like margarine."

"Not really."

"She never laughs properly and she spits on people's backs."

"She spits on people's backs?"

"Yes. I saw her and Marie doing it in the corridor. Only to fat people and Ann Barry." I think, *That sounds like something Alice would do.* Ann Barry has learning difficulties and often falls asleep while picking her nose. Alice takes photos.

Hattie rearranges herself. She rests her head on my chest.

I try to focus on the film.

I mentally Photoshop Aaron Mathews's face onto Leonardo DiCaprio's, and Alice's onto Kate Winslet's. I feel tiny bubbles of anger rising up from my ankles and bursting behind my eyes. I mentally encourage the plot of the film to change, abruptly and drastically, so that they both get beheaded by a rampaging murderer before kissing for the first time.

I feel heavy weather for thinking like that.

When Kate tries to suicide off the boat, we kiss. Hattie climbs on top of me. She's close, and I want her to be closer. I want her face to melt into my face, and I want my face to melt into Kate Winslet's face.

"You've got a boner."

"Do I? No, I don't." I try to nudge my boner to one side, but it's impossible because Hattie's sitting on top of it, looking down at me like I've committed a violent and calculated crime. She's pinning it down like a winning wrestler.

"Yes, you do. You haven't had one before."

I think, *Smackdown.*

"Yes, I have."

I think, *The Alice Gulf.*

"Not against my leg." She scratches her eyebrow. "It's because Alice doesn't matter anymore. We should stop. One of us could get attached."

"No, we won't. I will always never love you."

"Everything isn't you."

"What?"

She climbs off me and settles onto her back to watch the film. I don't understand. Leonardo is eating dinner with Kate and Kate's horrible boyfriend. They offer him caviar. I think, *Is caviar real?* You can probably get it at Waitrose. Alice's dad probably eats it on his Weetabix.

I'm hungry. I want to eat Hattie's sweet-corn fritters. How do I make her cook them?

"Leonardo's face looks great in this," I say. "It looks like a sweet-corn fritter."

I stare at Hattie.

"No, it doesn't."

"It looks great," I say. "Like a sweet-corn fritter."

"What are you talking about?"

"Can you cook sweet-corn fritters, please?"

Hattie sits up and looks at me. Her eyes have sad dogs behind them. She shakes her head. She picks up her shoes and walks out of the room and quietly closes the door. I pull the duvet over my head.

10

Amundsen watches the rest of *Titanic* with me, and we eat. Afterward, we watch a documentary about wild Alaskan salmon and fall asleep on the sofa. When I wake up, the sky's coming down a little and Amundsen's pacing in the kitchen. I attach his lead and we go into the Outside.

The sun is hiding behind swelling clouds. A girl on a bike is smoking. I can't see Mabel anywhere. I imagine her lying dead in the shower, with Mushroom kissing her folded ears and clambering across her back. I walk to the center of the field and sit down. I call Alice.

"Alice?" I say. "It's me."

"Etgar? Where are you? It's windy. I have to go in a minute."

"Go and eat a bag of dicks."

"What?"

"Sorry, nothing. Aslam told me to say that. I am breaking up with you." I look at Amundsen. He's being stroked by a man beneath an open golf umbrella.

"What? Etgar? Why? What's happened?"

"Because you lied about Aaron Mathews. You said he raped you with kisses but he didn't, you kissed each other, which I understand, because he is taller and more muscly and has more facial hair than me, but it's not okay to do that because you were my girlfriend and I was your boyfriend, and that isn't what girlfriends and boyfriends do."

There's a pause and Alice starts to cry. I thought I'd be crying but I'm not. A lot of bad things have happened in my head already, and now my eyes are empty.

"It wasn't like that," she says. "I can explain."

"You can explain to your mum." I don't know what that means.

"I was drunk. And you weren't there. I was being stupid. I thought you'd be kissing someone in Leicester."

"I was staying with my gran in Leicester." Amundsen comes to sit next to me. He drops his wet snout onto my shoulder. I imagine that he is my sidekick and Alice is an evil villain we need to defeat. I will hold her down by the wrists. Amundsen will tear off her head.

"Etgar?"

"Alice."

We'll play Frisbee with the severed head.

"I can't go to sixth form without you. I don't want to. Please."

When we're tired, I'll let Amundsen eat it.

"I'm still going to sixth form."

It will have the texture of underdone pork and taste faintly of garlic.

"You know what I mean."

He will give up after six bites.

"Then you shouldn't have handjobbed Aaron Mathews. Go back in time and hit him or something."

I don't want to tear off her head.

"I love you."

I want to kiss it.

"Do you?"

I want to rub my head against it.

"Yes."

Wait, I don't.

"I'm going to go now."

I don't know.

"Etgar, please."

"Sorry."

"I'll let you finger someone. Anyone you want."

"I don't want to finger anyone. You're the only person I want to finger."

"Then finger me."

"I don't know if I want to finger you anymore."

I hang up. I feel like a serious man in the emotional

climax of a film that ends with teary defeat. I wish this was in a film. I wish I was sitting on a sofa watching the film with Alice and eating Doritos and laughing. I'm not. I'm in the middle of a cold field with a stupid dog. There's nothing in the sky. There's no one else here. I lie down in the grass. I lie on my front. Amundsen lies next to me, our faces turned toward each other. He's panting. My heart is going triple-time. I know I definitely want to do something, but I don't know what the something is.

11

I type *severe depression* into Mum's computer. It says to eat vegetables and run around outside. I don't think I have that. I type *autism*. I don't have that either. I type *cancer*. I type *Alice Calloway is a piece of shit*. I type *how to disappear*. There are lots of people talking about throwing themselves off buildings or eating lots of acetaminophen or other painful-sounding activities that require courage and also a car.

The computer says that there's a forest in Japan where a lot of people go to kill themselves. They tie colored tape to trees and walk with it in their hands in case they stop wanting to disappear and need to find a way out. There's a lot of tape. The forest looks like a room in a museum filled with diagonal lasers to stop people from stealing things. Volunteers walk through the forest looking for dead bodies and for people who want to be dead bodies but aren't 100 percent sure yet. There are a lot of empty tents in the forest and old cars in the parking lot.

I imagine a film where two sad people meet in the forest and fall in love and leave the forest and are happy forever. The film would be a romantic comedy with a lot of jokes about dying. The tagline would be "Sometimes you find everything, when you've got nothing left to lose." The soundtrack would be Sigur Rós.

I wonder if I will ever fall in love like people do in films. I wonder if I will take girls out to dinner and invite them back to my house, then prematurely ejaculate into my well-ironed trousers.

Nothing is going to happen from now until forever.

I'm being melodramatic.

I'm hungry.

I eat a Ryvita cracker and check the computer. Macy's sent me an email. The subject line is *this was you*. There's an attachment. I download and open it. I'm looking at a large, pink dildo being held up to a webcam in the hand of a thin woman. The woman's fingernails are immaculately painted the color of black currant juice. The dildo is the length of both of my hands put together. I stretch out the waistband of my boxer shorts and look down at my dick. I sigh. She's online.

"I'm not that big," I say. "I'm not pink."

"Oh," she says. "It's not about length. This was a gift from my ex. It's about people."

"Oh. Yeah. Great. I fuck the woman too. I like looking at the woman in the face. I like looking at the woman in the eyes."

I have no idea what we are talking about.

"Mm. I think you'll like my eyes hehe."

"Me too."

"What color are yours? I couldn't see in the pic."

I stand up and walk over to the mirror and stare at myself.

"I'm not sure. Gray or blue or something."

"Metallic."

"I guess."

No. Absolutely not.

"Mm."

"Mm."

"Mm."

"Are you okay?"

"Yes. You?"

"I'm okay."

"You hard?"

No.

"Yes."

"I'm wet. I wish you were here."

"Me too."

"Are you in the office now?"

I look at Amundsen. He yawns.

"Yes," I say. "It's a nightmare. I wish I was tucked into a warm bed with you."

"Me too."

"I wish the bed was floating in the middle of the ocean."

"We could fuck each other all day."

"Birds would drop parcels of chocolate down to us."

"Hon, that sounds like heaven."

It sounds wildly dangerous.

It sounds better than anything happening here.

"I know."

"Do you have time to play?"

"I've got some work to do. And a meeting. Later I'll lock the door and we can do that."

"Okay. I'll be waiting."

"Okay."

I'm bored and I don't want to be anywhere, so I decide to walk to the corner shop for cider, because what else. I put Mum's coat on and apologize to Amundsen, who whines behind the front door like a child locked out of his parents' party.

It doesn't feel like a party in the Outside.

It feels heavy and cold.

The air smells of popcorn and dead leaves. Next to one house, it smells of roast dinner. I can see two people sitting down at a table inside. There are candles. I want to be inside with them. I want to eat roast dinner at a table with a girl and then sex the girl and fall asleep on her stomach.

Three men run the corner shop by my house. When I go inside, they're playing catch with rotten tomatoes. One of them nods at me. A tomato lands by my feet. I look down at it and panic. The cheap tract lighting highlights its misshapenness. The men are looking at me. Do I throw it or step over it or pick it up and eat it? I'm probably not supposed to eat it. I should make a joke. If I don't make a joke, then I'll look rude and offended. I'm not offended. It's only a tomato.

I throw the tomato to the nearest man.

I shout, "Beckham."

The man looks confused. I'm confused. I try to remember a better sporting fact than that David Beckham exists.

"Joking," I say, closing my eyes for a second and walking into the alcohol aisle. The men are looking at me and thinking about how stupid I am. They think I walk around shouting "Beckham" at everything. Maybe I should do that. That would be easier than trying to remain coherent.

Beckham.

White Ace is the most alcohol for the least amount of money. It's £3.89 for a three-liter bottle. That is enough for me to drink until sleeping isn't hard to do. It is enough for me to vomit in the morning and then drink a little more with breakfast. Hangovers don't matter if you are allowed to stay in bed or if your girlfriend has been kissing Aaron Mathews.

I pick up two cans of tripe and go to the counter. The man in front of me buys three porn magazines in gray plastic wallets. I briefly panic that I've somehow gone back in time to the '80s. AIDS is real again. My parents use swear words. Everything is grainy. Computers are houses.

I pay for my stuff with 20p coins and refuse a plastic bag. At the door, I turn around and say "Beckham." The men smile at me. They smile *Okay, that's great* smiles and I sink.

Alice Poem #2
Once there was an elephant mum and
the elephant mum had a baby and the baby
elephant had no legs and everyone called
it a retard and hit it with sticks and the mum
elephant ate the baby elephant and was Moby
Dick even real by the way Poems Are Gay and
Elephants
Are Gay and I want to wake up in yesterday and
FUCK YOU.

12

I'm indiscriminately slapping bushes as I walk past the repainted houses where young professionals with clean babies live. Sometimes I pull leaves off and throw them at other bushes. There are lights on in most of the houses. Soft, white IKEA lights looking over original floorboards and large televisions and full fruit bowls.

Someone's walking toward me.

He's looking down into his phone.

It's the Tiger.

I stop. I don't know what to do. He looks up. My body stops working. It won't do anything. It has fallen asleep. My body often fails to be a real asset to my brain, I feel.

He walks toward me, slowly and unevenly, sliding his phone into the pocket of his quilted jacket.

"All right," he says. He doesn't say it like a question. I nod, and he hits me.

I can tell that he's going to hit me, so I lean into the punch, effectively reducing its potential for serious damage. This is something I learned from Dad. Thanks, Dad.

He hits me in the eye that he didn't hit me in last time. Is that considerate? I can't tell. I tip backward but don't fall over. My body has started working again. It turns around and runs. It runs past the lit-up windows and the shop and the hairdresser, hugging the green plastic bottle of cider. The Tiger is behind me. His feet clap the ground so fast it sounds like sleet. He catches my collar and I stop. I shake off his hand. I face him.

"Wait," I say. "Wait. Stop fighting me. I'll give you ten pounds."

"I don't want ten quid," he says. He's out of breath. "I want to fuck you in."

"You're going to bum me?"

"Fuck off, am I."

"Wait, are you?"

"No."

Another gap of silence opens between us.

"You want to talk to God?" I say. "Let's go see him together. I've got nothing better to do."

And I hit him. I'm amazed at my hands. I think, *Congratulations, me.* It isn't a hard punch, but it's definitely a punch. He doesn't move at all and doesn't look hurt, only surprised and slightly angry.

"Stop fighting me," I say again. "Don't fight me anymore."

"You hit me."

"You hit me first."

"Whatever."

"Wait, if I let you punch me in the face, can I go? Or I'll lie down and you can kick me. I don't care. You choose."

"No."

"What do you mean, no?" I lie down on the pavement and curl into a ball. I look into the nighttime I've made inside of my elbows. I'm safe. I'm lying in Mum's womb as she reclines on the sofa, watching *Escape to the Sun* and being brought cups of ginger tea. "Kick me. It doesn't matter. Beckham."

"I'm not going to kick you. Get up."

"No. You'll just punch me. Kick me now. Wherever you want."

"Get up, you twat."

"Kick me in the head. Go on."

"Stop being a prick."

"Kick me. Beckham. Fuck me in. Bum me. Do whatever."

"I'm not going to bum you. Stop saying that."

"Break my spine. Sit on me. Jump on me. Bite off my ear."

"Just get up. Jesus."

"Will you punch me if I get up?"

"Stand up and give me the ten quid."

"Okay."

I stand up and give him the ten pounds. He looks me in the eyes. I look him in the eyes too. His face isn't scary like Aaron Mathews's. Maybe because I'm not imagining it nuzzling Alice's vagina. What if they had a threesome? A Manson family drugs orgy. Joking. His face isn't scary, because it looks like Simba's.

"You can have it back," he says. "I don't want it."

I don't take it. I turn around and walk back toward home. I walk slowly and count my steps, making sure not to stand on sets of three drains because Aslam says that's bad luck, and I don't want more of that, or I do, or it doesn't matter.

PART 2

Wet

13

I came home from school, made tea, and sat with Mum while she watched the news. The news said that young people were stabbing each other. In the gut and in the face and in the heart. They were dying. It showed pictures of their knives. All of the knives were bigger than mine. Some flicked out of their handles. Some were the length of babies. One was a samurai sword. One was a machete. I buried the butter knife by the dead apple tree in our garden and took a bread knife instead.

They found the second weapon at school one day when Ellen Kane's christening necklace went missing. She had taken it off for art. Mrs. Layton wouldn't let anyone leave the room until someone owned up and gave it back. No one owned up and gave it back.

Mrs. Layton told us to put our bags on the table. She came to us one by one and performed thorough and invasive searches. My hands were dripping. I asked if I could go to the toilet. Mrs. Layton said to wait. I said I really needed to go. She said I really needed to wait. I said, "I'm literally going to shit myself" and she gave me a detention. When she got to my bag, my knees were bouncing like basketballs and I was trying not to cry.

"Get away," I said. "I know my rights. You need a warrant for that."

I had been listening to a lot of Jay-Z.

She shouted. She made me stand in a corner.

Then the bread knife appeared in her hand.

Then I was sitting in the principal's office, next to Mum, holding toilet paper against my eyes, promising that I was not planning to do a murder.

"But why do you have it?" Mr. Keating said. He was rubbing his chin. "That's what I want to know."

"I don't know."

"What are you scared of?"

"Just scared."

Three days later, a policeman came to our house. He smelled of chewing gum, hair gel, and too much deodorant. His hands were tiny and hardly moved. I talked at them, not at his face.

"You're not in trouble," he said. "But we need you to understand how serious this is." He blinked. "It's very serious." (Later, I found out that school had suspected Dad of fingering me while I slept.)

He asked me what I was planning to do with the knife. I said I was planning to defend myself. He told me that adults were there to protect me, and that no one can hurt me in school. I asked if he'd ever heard of Columbine. He said that sort of thing only happens in America and he told me not to do it again and he went away.

"There's nothing to be afraid of," Mum said. "You know you can talk to me about anything, darling." I turned the TV to BBC1 because I thought it would be the news, but it wasn't, it was a program about antiques. I locked myself in the bathroom and lay in the empty bathtub for two hours, picturing myself alone in a spaceship, surrounded by slowly spinning purple galaxies.

Mum reacted by saying that I could do martial arts. Ben Wheelan said there were kung fu monks who can kill you without even touching you. That sounded like something I wanted to do. I went through the phone book and found a place run by a woman. I trusted women more. They can't do rapes and their hands are smoother. I stopped going after two sessions because none of the moves seemed like they could beat a knife or a gun.

Dad reacted by giving me a used copy of a book called *The Worst-Case Scenario Survival Handbook*. It was supposed to make me less anxious. I memorized everything in it. It didn't make me less anxious. It brought to my attention the almost endless amount of potentially dangerous situations I had to be anxious about. It said about how to deliver babies and cope with parachutes that won't open. It talked about how to act while on the roof of a moving train.

The school year ended on a day without clouds, and I stopped seeing Ben Wheelan. I got into a secondary school with an entrance exam. He got into a secondary school for people who sometimes hit other people.

I spent the summer collecting slugs in plastic takeaway cartons, reading *The Worst-Case Scenario Survival Handbook,* and stealing Dad's beers.

14

At home, I watch my face in the bathroom mirror. It looks red and a little confused. There are no bruises yet. There will be. I'm Natasha Bedingfield. It will be okay. Mum will believe me when I tell her it's from walking into a lamppost. Dad will think it's from fighting and he won't say anything, but he'll secretly be imagining the triumphant victory of his only son. A victory in which I break bones and spit blood between punches.

I splash myself with water and go to watch television on the sofa with Amundsen. I fill a pint glass with cider. There's a film on where Daniel Craig and Jamie Bell do Polish accents and captain a group of Jews who are hiding from the Nazis in a deep forest. They build huts and steal food and argue. There's a lot of arguing. There are a lot of guns being fired and hungry people with mud-speckled faces. Normally, I only like films where nothing bad happens. Where you know that no one will die or get severely maimed or starve. Films like *Love Actually* and *Bridget Jones's Diary*. There's no way that Bridget Jones would ever be raped and left for dead, so I didn't feel anxious during it. I felt calm with alternating periods of amusement and sadness.

I like the film about the Jews, though. I start to pretend that I'm one of them. I'm taking lookout duty late at night. I'm breaking into the ghetto to let the others know they can join us. I'm shooting Nazis in their cars and celebrating afterward. It's tough, but it's what we have to do to survive.

Eat.

Hide.

Kill Nazis.

When it ends, I'm alone with a sleeping Amundsen, very drunk, and increasingly aware that I'm not the leader of any kind of uprising.

Macy's online.

I carry the computer upstairs and climb into bed with it. I lock Amundsen out. I pull off my trousers and one sock, and bring the duvet up to my chin.

"Hi," I say. "How are you?"

"Hi. Did you get caught in the office?"

"Almost. It was close. My boss was talking to me and my dick was out."

"That's hot."

"Yeah. And dangerous. I could have lost my job, which I need to support myself and so on."

"It was fun."

"I wish you were here. I wish someone was here. Or I was somewhere else."

"Bad day?"

"No," I say. "Yes." I got punched in the face and mugged, quietly, like an elderly person giving out their credit card details over the phone. "Sometimes I think about finding a small, dark space and climbing in, and never coming out. Not for food or water or people or anything. And I die in the space, but it's okay, because it's just in the space." I'm drunk. I shouldn't have said that.

"I think about that too, but then I think about angry hands reaching in to pull me out, and it seems worse than never going in."

"I wish people would let other people hide."

"I've got kids, hon. I know." I try to imagine being permanently tied to two miniature humans who require constant amusement and affection. I picture myself lightly holding a roll of yellow tape, walking between trees, testing the strengths of various low branches.

"That's horrible."

"Haha."

"That you always have to be responsible, I mean."

"It's like everything's narrowed down to right now,

and you can't do what you want. It's like there's this point where doing what you want starts being selfish."

"What do you want to do?"

"Anything. I don't know. Go somewhere hot and exotic, where I don't know anyone. Somewhere with palm trees and cocktails. Learn the language. Get a bar job. Sleep whenever I want."

"That sounds nice. We should do that."

"I wish."

"Your kids will be fine. Kids grow up quickly now. When you leave, they'll invent a new kind of social networking and become billionaires."

"Haha."

I don't know what to say.

"Where are they?"

"Bed."

"That's great."

"I think we should do a voice chat," she says.

"Do you?"

"Would be hot."

"I think my mic is broken. Or I don't have one. I don't know."

"Let's try."

"Maybe later."

Macy is calling you. Oh God. She'll be able to tell. She'll realize that I'm a child masquerading as someone worth talking to and she'll call the police. I'm shaking. I'm drunk. I press *accept.* A female voice comes into my room. It's gentle and perfect, like the voiceover on a tourism advert for a country where people take afternoon naps and eat outdoors.

I'm scared. The voice says my name. It says, "Are you there?"

"My mic isn't working," I type. "I am shouting into it."

"Yes, it is," the voice says. "I can hear you typing."

"Oh," I say out loud. "Sorry. I was scared. I haven't ever done this."

"Your accent is sexy."

"Yours is nice."

"Don't be scared. I won't bite." She laughs. I try to laugh with her but it sounds quiet and stuttered. "You're nervous. Relax."

"I'm trying."

"Big scary yacht thieves have nothing to be afraid of."

I laugh.

"They get scared of extremely attractive Scottish women."

"I'll protect you from any if I see them."

"Ahoy! You's a one."

"Sorry?"

"Um. Nothing."

"Will you describe where you are again?"

"Okay, wait. I'm going to carry you downstairs. I need to get another drink," I say.

"I'll get one too."

I pick up the laptop and push open my door. Amundsen's waiting outside. He rears up and presses his paws into my belly. I try to bat him away without making any sound. It doesn't work. I whisper his name and flick his ears.

"Who are you talking to, hon?"

"No one."

"Who is it?"

"It's my dog. Say hi, Amundsen." I let him lick my hand next to the computer.

"Aw. Cute. Okay, getting a drink too."

I put the laptop on the living room table and look through the alcohol cabinet. I'm bored of White Ace. Dad's Famous Grouse is almost gone. There are two more bottles of red wine, half a bottle of Baileys, something lumpy and made of coconut, something called grenadine, sloe gin, sloe vodka, sloe tequila (all made by Dad for Christmas), and port. I decide I want red wine. People like red wine. One of the bottles has a church on it, the other has autumn leaves. I choose leaves, because churches are for people who are dying or dead.

"Have you got one?"

I jump. I forgot there was a woman here.

"I've got one. Have you?"

"Yes. Some good Shiraz."

I look at the label on mine.

"I've got some great Cabernet Sauvignon."

She laughs. "You mean Cabernet Sauvignon, hon."

She says it like Cah-bern-ey Soh-vin-yon. I said it like Cab-er-net Soh-vig-non. I said it correctly, I feel.

"It's how we say it down here. Aren't cultural differences so interesting?"

She laughs again. "Cute," she says.

"Um."

"Tell me what it's like now. You aren't in your study?"

I hold the bottle between my legs and uncork it. I take a deep swig. "I'm lying on the sofa in my living room. My living room is bare wooden floorboards, a Persian rug, a large television, and some erotic statues and other sexy things. The sofa is huge. It's a seven-person sofa." That sounds too big. It sounds creepy. "A seven-children sofa," I say. "That's a joke I like to make. I don't actually have seven children. I don't have any children." I think, *Slow down. Relax. Nothing bad is going to happen.*

"Haha. Okay. It sounds pretty."

"Your turn."

"Okay, well, I'm lying in bed with my black lace bra and panties on. I can see a few stars outside and what I think is a gibbous moon."

I have a boner already. Gibbous moon. That's so sexy. I want to tell her to make sex noises, but she is a fully grown woman so I have to be slow and seductive like in films. I have to make her feel special. I want to. I feel somehow that she feels like I do and that is how we've ended up in the same room.

"That sounds great."

"What are you wearing?"

I blink and flex my toes. I'm wearing gray, paint-flecked jogging bottoms and a T-shirt that says Malta over a cartoon palm tree.

"White jockeys and a dressing gown."

"Maybe you should take it off."

"Okay," I say, my voice sliding up. I pull the jogging bottoms down to my ankles and cup my balls. "I did it."

"I wish I could see. Will you send a pic?"

No.

"Yes. Will you?"

"Of course."

I turn on the webcam and step back to look at myself in the screen. I undress to my boxer shorts. My body is pale and lacking in muscle definition. It isn't short, but my BMI is noticeably below average. When we have to line up in height order for school photos, I fall around the middle.

By rolling my shoulders forward, tensing my neck and pushing out my jaw, I make my body look more substantial and alluring. It still doesn't seem particularly alluring. It seems upsetting. I want Tim Gunn to appear and tell me how beautiful I am. I want him to introduce me to new ways of thinking that make me shine like the star I am.

I'm stupid.

I'm nothing.

I'm a slashed hovercraft, stuck in marshes, miles from the nearest town.

Macy's the nearest town.

Macy's Scotland.

"Did you take one?"

"Yes. Did you?"

"Sending."

My dick beats. The woman in the picture has large breasts and well-distributed curves. Shafts of toned muscle divide her skin like sand dunes. She must work out on a daily basis. She must be capable of prolonged and rigorous sexual activity. Once, I had sex with Alice for forty-five minutes. I was extremely drunk and failed to cum.

"You're so sexy," I say. I have never said *sexy* in a serious context before, and it makes me choke a little. I'm a person who says *sexy* now. I'm a person who calls other people sexy. *A little more wine, please, sexy. Okay, sexy, here you go.* "You must work out."

"Thanks. Yeah. I like to run. Send yours."

"I look stupid in comparison. I don't run. I should run. My body is ugly."

"We all think that sometimes, trust me."

"Okay."

I send it.

"You're sexy too. I love skinny guys."

And children?

"Thanks."

"So are you going to turn up here any time soon?"

"Um. I don't think so. Scotland seems far."

She laughs.

"Oh, you meant . . . Yes. I am. I am lying underneath your bed. I am pressing my face against the shape of your body through this mattress."

"Come up and kiss me."

"Okay."

"Are you hard?"

"Yes."

"I'm wet already. I can feel it through the lace. I'm wet."

"I can feel it too. Against my knee." What? Against my knee. Jesus. Knees aren't sexy. Say a different body part. "And my thumb." Good one.

"Take off my bra."

"Your nipples are hard. I'm sucking and biting them. I'm squeezing your ass." *Ass* is another very difficult word to say. *Ass. Ass. Ass.* I need to practice that.

"Your balls are in my hand. They feel full."

"They are full."

A bit gross, but fine. Go with it.

"I've turned you over and pinned you down."

"Okay."

"Taken off my panties and climbed onto your face."

"Your pussy is in my face now."

I give up.

"It's so wet."

"My tongue is inside of you. It is flicking against that bean at the top." I can hear a wet slapping sound coming from Macy. The same sound is also coming from me.

"Mm."

"I am holding your thighs and rolling you back and forth."

"Fucking eat my pussy, you pathetic asshole."

"Um. I'm not really into that either."

"Oh, I just thought . . . because you did it. Okay. Keep eating."

She's moaning. She's moaning in long, low bursts, like a zombie. There are no sounds coming from my mouth. I don't make sex noises. I'm anxious about sounding retarded.

"Your turn," she says. "I'm kissing from your chin down. All the way down your naked body. Down your chest and your belly. To your hard cock."

"Great."

I'm terrible at every kind of sex ever invented.

"Do you have hair?"

"Yes."

Not really.

"Good. I don't like men who look like babies. I'm licking around your huge balls. Kissing up your shaft. Taking it in my mouth."

Why does she want me to have big balls so much? It doesn't matter, I guess. I can have whatever she wants me to have. I can be her dream man.

"Yes, my giant veiny balls. It feels good." I make my hand go slower. I'm scared of cumming. "On my massive balls. Thanks."

"Taking you all the way into my throat."

"I am pushing you off and bending you over."

"Fuck."

"Pulling your legs apart and pushing myself into you."

"Fuck, hon. It feels amazing."

"Putting my fingers between your fingers and my face into your hair."

"I'm pushing against you with my ass. Faster."

"Okay."

"Go faster. Fuck. Harder."

"I am fucking you."

"Harder."

"I'm trying."

"Harder."

"I'm honestly trying my best."

"Fuck me."

"I am."

I'm not.

"Fuck."

"Fuck."

"Fuck."

"Yes."

"Jesus."

I cum. I pull off the sock and throw it at the television. Macy does a high-pitched moan and a sigh. I go to shout "spilled wine" and slam the computer, but she says something that makes me stop. She says, "Oh, I wish you could snuggle through the computer."

There's a pause. We're panting.

"You can sort of fuck. But you can't hug afterward. You're alone. Even if you forgot for a second." She's talking in between fast, windy breaths. "It's like, I don't know. Hon, that was great. I love doing this with you."

"Me too. It's good. I've got to go. Um. I've got to do something."

"Do you have to?"

"I'm sorry."

"Email me. Please."

"I will."

"Good-bye, hon."

"Bye."

I roll a cigarette, light it, and sit on the living room carpet hugging myself. Why did I go? Macy's nice. She doesn't make me feel small. She wants to hide too. The Alice Gulf. I push my eyes into my arm. They're heavy. Amundsen wakes up, shakes himself, and comes over to put his tongue in my ear. My arms fall and I turn to face him. He licks my bruises.

15

I finish the bottle of wine in the bath, surrounded by bubble clouds, loudly singing "Drop the World" to a rubber duck. I hold my breath underwater, pretending that I'm a giant squid at the bottom of the blackest ocean. The part so deep that it will never meet the sun, only hear about it in whispers from passing whales. No human will ever see me. I will die, and my bulbous body will be picked apart by creatures that have not yet been discovered.

There's an orgy happening in my head.

Alice sucking Aaron Mathews's dick. Aaron Mathews fisting Alice. Alice sliding a finger into Aaron Mathews's ass. Aaron Mathews enjoying it. Aaron Mathews cumming on Alice's face. Alice enjoying it. Aaron Mathews being immediately ready to begin again. A third person entering the room. The third person being invited to participate.

I wish I was the third person.

No, I don't.

I'm drinking neat gin.

Staring at the ceiling.

I slip twice when I get out of the bath, cracking my head against the sink. Everything's being dragged down. Everything's being weighed down by the weight of Alice's disappearance. She didn't disappear. She made me make her disappear. She's gone. I'm one human in the world. I don't want to be one human in the world. I want to be Alice and Etgar in the world.

I don't dry myself. I climb straight into old clothes.

I take £30 from the box in my parents' bedroom, drink more cider, and leave. Doing the key is hard, so I leave the door unlocked. The rain outside has settled in small pools dotted along the pavement. It's half-light. A single gray bird loiters by the roots of a tree. I scream and chase it into the sky. I follow the street down and to the right, onto Denton Lane, where there are three shops the color of old fax machines. One's a dry cleaner. One's a hairdresser. One's Shanghai Palace.

The waitress who seats me is familiar from times I've gotten takeout. She is short and perfect-looking in the way that any young female who is not Alice is now perfect-looking. I want to ask if she'll come home with me, to build a blanket castle and drink rum and watch Judd Apatow films. The thing that makes me do heavy weather most is when you see someone and you can tell they want to be not alone and you know you want to be not alone but you can't be not alone together because of things like how she's forty-two and you're fifteen, or how she's got kids and your mum's waiting for you at home. That's what makes me do heavy weather the most. It's fucking retarded.

I don't say anything.

I let her direct me to a table next to the tank of clownfish.

I do an Irish accent. I say "Top of the morning to you" in it. I immediately feel severely retarded and like I want to climb into bed and never climb out.

"Are you okay?" the waitress says.

"Yes," I say. I'm still doing the accent.

"Yes?"

My body sags. Bodies aren't supposed to be this heavy. "No," I say. "Alice lied about being raped with kisses by Aaron Mathews. He's got tribal tattoos. He punched me and I don't know what to do. I want to get drunk. I want to disappear." The fish in the tank drift past each other like blimps. They don't fight and don't lie and are never alone. "Yes," I say.

"To drink?" she says.

"To drinking," I say. "I mean yes. Drinks. Wine. Gay wine. Rosé."

She nods and disappears.

I think about Macy. I imagine her having a midlife crisis that manifests itself in the form of a large, expensive coffee machine. I imagine her worrying about her children being bullied because their shoes don't light up. I imagine her hiding under a duvet and sighing and masturbating over me, a twenty-six-year-old mortgage broker who owns a briefcase and knows the rules of golf.

The wine arrives. I pour a glass and down it. I order beef in green pepper and black bean sauce, three bowls of chips, and prawn crackers. When the prawn crackers come, I line four up on the table and give them names. I eat the Alice one. It tastes stale and chewy. I move the Aslam cracker into the gap. I eat it too.

*

There isn't a fortune in my fortune cookie. There's a bad joke: *What do you get when you cross a creek and a river? Wet feet.*

*

The waitress wakes me up and asks me to leave. I tuck the £30 into her breast pocket, flatten my hair, and go outside. At home, I collapse and open the computer. There's an email waiting. From Macy.

<To: etgarfamousrapper@hotmail.co.uk>
RE: something

Etgar,

I hope this doesn't sound weird, and I'm sorry I didn't say something before, I was worried that it would sound weird, and now it definitely does sound weird. If you think it's weird, forget I said anything. Please, hon. I really enjoy playing with you and don't want to fuck it up.

I'm coming to London in two days.

It's for a business meeting that's been planned for months. Meeting retailers and that sort of thing. But if you had any free time, I'd love to meet up. I know we barely know each other but I've been thinking about you. I've been thinking about what it would be like to touch you.

Actually, since your first picture I imagined us meeting in London when I came for this meeting. I imagined you meeting me off the plane, and fucking me in the train station toilets.

My train gets in at six in the evening. I don't have any meetings that day so maybe we could spend the night together then.

Talk later,
Macy

PS: Attached something to prove something.

It's an .mp4 attachment. I download and play it. Macy's face fills my screen. She stares into her computer. She's doing a *don't be afraid of me* smile.

"Etgar," she says. "I'm not a man. I promise."

She's wearing a thin, white vest top, and the wine-color straps of her bra are visible. There are smudges that look like oil under her eyes. She presses a key and disappears.

I stare at my hands. I want mouths to appear in my hands and I want the mouths to talk and tell me what to do. Would she be able to tell I wasn't a mortgage broker? Wait, what? I can't go to London. I can't. I could. The money Gran left me. I can't go and have sex with a woman from the Internet. It wouldn't work. Amundsen's here. I'm staying. I'll tell her I'm busy. I'll tell her it's mortgage-broking season. Everyone wants their mortgages broken this time of year. I'm swamped.

Do something.

I go into the kitchen, fill a pint glass with water, and down it. There's half of the cider left. I refill the pint glass with that. My stomach panics and settles. Amundsen comes in from the garden. He's holding a dead rat in his mouth. His snout is damp with red. The rat lands between my feet and Amundsen sits back, wagging his tail, eyes wide with pride.

"Can we just—" I say. "Can you put that somewhere else?"

He doesn't put it somewhere else.

"I'm proud of you. Now go and eat it or something."

He doesn't eat it. I pick it up by its tail and carry it through to the garden, throwing it as far as my arm will throw. It cartwheels in the air and lands near the compost heap.

16

My phone wakes me up. Mum. I feel bloated and brain-dead. I'm on the sofa, under a yellow towel, two empty crisp packets, and Amundsen's forelegs. The sky looks like it's mid-afternoon and verging on rain. I press *accept*.

"Hi," Dad says.

"Hi, Dad." It's unusual for Dad to talk on the phone. He says it's dishonest, and that there are too many secret rules, like how you have to wait for the other person to say hi first.

"Your mum made me call."

"What's she doing?"

"I'm not entirely sure. She appears to be playing some sort of coin game with Alena's family. A kind of flicking game. They're flicking the coins."

I relocate to the windowsill. Amundsen rises, sniffs his paw, and lies back down. "What's Alena like?"

Dad makes rustling sounds. His breathing deepens. "They're too close. I'll tell you when I get back."

"Yes or no that they're hilarious together?"

"Absolutely yes."

"Okay." I picture Uncle Michael in a tuxedo, awkwardly pushing his mouth against the mouth of a woman who doesn't understand anything he says.

"Did you kill or set fire to anything?"

"Not yet."

"And you're okay?"

"I'm fine."

"Should I check anything else?"

"I don't know. About Amundsen maybe."

"Did you walk it?"

"Yes."

"Okay, I'm going now."

He hangs up.

I stand at the window and pinch my cheeks. Amundsen nuzzles the backs of my knees. A cornflake-colored squirrel darts along the branches of our elm tree, shakes its head, and disappears behind a cloud of leaves.

"Breakfast."

In the kitchen, I make coffee, put toast in, and fill a bowl with dry dog food. Amundsen eats quickly and runs several laps of the garden. I butter the toast, pour out coffee, and arrange everything on the table.

I open Mum's computer and read *Guardian* articles about rape law, piracy, and ecological disaster. Heavy, distant things that will never enter this kitchen. I sip coffee. It tastes like canned soup but makes the tiny people in my body start to sit up and yawn and add milk to cereal.

Sarah Wakely is sick and tired of being sick and tired.

Elliot Venn loves fat cocks and not logging off fb.

Thayyab Ahmed is starting pre-drinks a little early methinks.

I click on Alice.

She's sitting on the deck of a catamaran, cradling a cocktail glass and smiling. She's by a boy the color of hazelnuts. His hand is around her shoulder and his fingers are dangling by the pits of her collarbones. I go to the alcohol cabinet, take another red wine, and decide to finish it all on the sofa while blowing saliva bubbles and watching *Storage Wars*.

17

The wind in the Outside has muscles. It's kicking at the branches of trees and hurling leaves at windows. There's a little water in the wind. A man passes me, carrying four Tesco bags fat with food. I run and fall. My knees burn. The man turns his head and keeps walking. I get up and keep running. I don't look into the houses. I run and my head gets hot. I'm angry.

Fuck you, Alice.

Fuck everything.

I sat next to you in church while you bit your fingers and cried. I stayed awake with you watching documentaries about potential afterlives. I carried your dad to his car. I epilated your bum. I shampooed your hair and painted your toenails, and now you're sunbathing with hazelnuts.

You kissed Aaron Mathews.

You held his dick in your hand.

Fuck you.

I collapse onto the grass at the park, in the same spot Aslam and I fell after the party.

After I tried to hit someone for you.

The tall buildings are capped with bright lights. Yellow and orange and red. The broad cement shoulders of the hospital are glowing. There's half a moon and thin strings of cloud. A plane cuts diagonally through them.

I call Alice.

"I'm calling to say you're a massive stupid walrus bitch."

"Etgar?"

"Stupid sea animal, go back to the sea."

"Etgar, please." Her voice wobbles.

"You ruin everything."

"Let me talk." It sounds like her cheeks are filled with water.

She's crying. I am too.

"Manson family sexy orgy with hazelnuts."

"What?"

"I know everything."

"What is everything?"

"Fuck you. I'm so sad."

"I am too."

"You're just sad you got caught. You got fingered and then sad. I just got sad. I want to be fingered by Aaron

Mathews's great hands that he punched my face with. He put his hand in your vag then punched my face with it. Fuck you." She's crying. I'm carrying on. "He punched me with your vagina and infidelity. I thought you were Alice, but you're not. You're something else. You're a walrus, and I hate you."

"Etgar." Her voice is small and wet.

"Etgar. Etgar. Etgar. Etgar. Etgar. Etgar. Etgar is hanging up the phone now, bye forever."

I stand up and pull at my hair. Clumps of it come out in my hands. My eyes blur. A police car runs past, and for a second everything is blue.

18

Two days before the start of secondary school, I Googled *how to shave* and cut my chin so deep it made me dizzy. I was eleven.

I went in for the first two days, felt like a coin lost down a sofa, and stopped going. I didn't like being on the smallest team in a school of towering boys. The boys didn't look like boys. They looked like lions next to Dad, and the girls looked like models with real breasts and painted fingernails. They were not mums.

For three months, I missed fifty percent of school. Dad left the house at seven. Mum at eight. I carried my duvet downstairs, lay on the sofa, and watched documentaries about natural disasters, genocide, and notorious serial killers. I went up to the loft and sorted through Dad's old records. I sold several of them on eBay and spent the money on Lili Six, sensuous massage in the comfort of your own home. I didn't have any sensuous massages in the comfort of my own home. Lili repeatedly called school and told them I had a bug/food poisoning/tonsillitis. She explained that I was born prematurely and so was prone to sickness. Lili called me "chick" in the mornings when we talked over the phone. She told me about premiership football scandals and I told her about Ted Bundy.

Eventually someone, somewhere, became suspicious, and school called one evening while Mum and Dad were in the living room watching *Casualty* and eating After Eights. They made me come downstairs and sit between them on the sofa. I didn't feel scared. I felt calm. My parents don't shout. They used to, when they still had sex, but stopped when they realized every argument ended the same way, with everything being fine.

"Are you being bullied?"

"Are you stressed?"

"Are you gay?"

A pause.

"Why would being gay mean skipping school?"

"It's a tough thing to come to terms with." Dad blinks and pulls his earlobe. "Very daunting." Mum stares at him.

"I'm not gay."

Dad has been suggesting this on a regular basis since

I was nine. He doesn't know how to react to male humans who are scared of things. He thinks that being scared is for women, gays, and the under-nines.

"It's okay if you are."

"Well, I'm not."

"Well, you can be."

"Thanks, Dad."

I had to go to school every day after that, otherwise they said they'd expel me and I'd move to a school with metal detectors and drug dogs. I did all of the work we were given quietly and quickly. I got good marks for Mum. I didn't care about good marks. I cared about bed and beer and Daniel Clowes. I spent a lot of time in the places people who don't have anywhere to go spend their time.

I met Sam in the toilet at lunchtime. He was sitting in a cubicle with his laptop, playing online poker and eating Haribo.

I met Aslam in the trees by the bottom of the field. We were both there to smoke. He gave me some of his beer and told me about a guy who made a porn with a girl but then he cut the girl up and had sex with the different parts.

I met Hattie in the library. She was by the reference books, reading *Ariel* and sniffing. I thought about maybe fingering her until she introduced me to James.

We started doing breaktimes together under a spruce tree next to the language block.

Alice didn't appear for another year. When she did, it was at the bottom of Chris McDowell's garden, midway through a party he was holding while his mum took his dad to London for a kidney operation. I was nauseous. I was looking for somewhere to hide.

"Hi," I said.

"Hello."

"I'm Etgar."

"I know. You're friends with Aslam. He called Eliza fat once. I punched him." I sat down in the grass next to her. Not too close. In case she hit me. I remembered the Eliza Incident. I remembered she's called Alice Calloway and she's in the year below us and she's severely attractive. I remembered Aslam's eye looked like a pork scratching.

"Ah," I said. "Sometimes he does-a not-a do-a the thinking."

"Was that an Italian accent?"

"No," I said. "Yes. Um. Why are you out here?"

"I came with Lydia, but she's getting with someone. I don't really know anyone else I want to talk to."

"Do you want me to go?"

"Are you going to rub your face against my tits and shout 'huzzah huzzah'?"

"No," I say. "Probably not. I'm not even-a doing the talking well. Sorry. I'm drunk."

"Are you the one that hides in closets?"

"No, that's Sam. He's not hiding. He just gets tired."

"Cool."

We stayed where we were and talked. We talked about who did the motorboating (Ellis Langton) and who shat themselves on the 86 and who had a Pokemon tattoo on their calf. We talked about school. We talked about which teacher is gay and which teacher had been castrated and which teacher got drunk and did anal with a year eleven on the Paris trip. We talked about Vonnegut. We talked about the Olsen twins. We talked about Slipknot.

Alice wasn't scary. She was good at doing talking. When I asked her about something she asked me about the something too, and she didn't stop until I gave an opinion that wasn't beige. I don't know why. She liked to talk about things other people think are disgusting. She'd read *Wetlands*. We thought the same things were gay.

"Wait here," she said. She got up and went. I thought, *She's definitely not going to come back. I was too boring. She's going upstairs to sit on the face of a boy more muscular and emotionally mature than me. I should have told jokes. I should have flexed.*

She came back.

She put her legs on my legs and lay back and twisted off the lid of a miniature bottle of rosé with her teeth.

"Gay wine," she said.

I've been picked for a team, I thought. *I'm on a team now.*

We finished the wine in silence, went upstairs, and lay in the bathtub, trying to make each other happy with our hands. I wasn't anxious about doing it wrong, because Alice told me exactly how to not do it wrong. It isn't about how many fingers you can get in and it isn't about how fast you can make those fingers work. She was the first girl to give me a blowjob without painfully plowing my dick skin with her teeth.

At 1:00, loud sounds happened downstairs. We followed them and they led to Aslam, standing at the front door, shrugging at two flustered parents.

"I heard there was a cocktail of drugs," the mum said.

"There isn't a 'cocktail of drugs.' Honestly, it's boring as shit." He tilted his head. "Did Martin tell you that? He's pissed because someone made him drink piss. There aren't any drugs. Look at my pupils." He moved his face very close to the woman's face.

"Get away from me," the mum said.

"Get away from her," the dad said.

"No need to be rude."

"I'll call the police."

"Help, police, some young people are in a house together and one of them tried to show me his beautiful emerald eyes."

The woman snorted. She grabbed her husband and turned and left.

"Martin's gay," Aslam shouted.

I kicked him. "Leave them alone."

"They're dicks. And you're a massive spastic."

"Do you have drugs left?"

"A bit."

"Bathroom."

Alice came with us to crowd around a toilet on the third floor. Aslam apologized for the Eliza Incident. She was in every bathroom after that. She was in my bedroom, Aslam's summerhouse, the days when I hid from school, and under the spruce tree.

19

"Fuck off," I say, hitting Amundsen in the nose and rolling over. My head is internally bleeding. My throat has been clawed by cats. "Amundsen, fuck off."

"Excuse me," a man's voice says. I blink and open my eyes. I'm underneath a bright turquoise sky. A confused black Doberman is watching me, tongue flapping out of the corner of its mouth. I look at my hands. They're panda hands. "Are you okay, young man?" I sit up. The man's eyebrows are bent into a *V*. "Is there someone I can call?"

I shake my head. "I'm sorry," I say. "For hitting your dog."

"Are you sure there's no one I can call?"

"No. Thank you. I'm okles dokles." I pinch my hands. "Okey dokey. It's okay. I'm okay. Okay?"

I stand up and fall to one side. The man takes hold of my arm and rights me. I thank him and run. My legs are foam. They pull me to the living room sofa and give up. The house was unlocked. All of the lights are on. Amundsen is asleep in the armchair. He's done more shits. I don't care. He can do as many shits as he likes. He should shit. He should keep shitting until everything is covered in a layer of shit sitting like thick ash on me and the house, stuck here in Pompeii.

Bile tides rise and fall in my neck. There's a stagnant pool of water burping in my belly. It's going to come up. Is it? Vomiting might be good, I feel. Or it might be like uncorking a bottle. I might keep vomiting until there's nothing left. Mum will find my body lying like a punctured balloon by the bath.

I make coffee with the French press, adding an extra spoonful of coffee and not knowing why. It's not that I want to be awake. I want to be asleep. Amundsen doesn't. He's kissing the mud stains around my ankles and doing contented dog sounds. He wants tripe, and I give him some, then let him out into the garden to be a detective questioning the weeds and leaves.

I get into bed and under the duvet. I don't want to be woken up by unfamiliar dogs in wet parks. I want to be woken up by quietly attractive women with Nesquik tea and athletic physiques.

<To: macyishiding@gmail.com>
RE: London

Macy,

It's not weird. Don't worry. You're coming to London for a meeting and that's where I definitely am. I want to see you too. Tell me where your meeting is the day after and I'll book us a hotel. I'd say we could stay at mine but renovations are being done and everything's messy. I'll find a good hotel. We can have dinner there. Maybe see a show or something afterward.

We're actually going to meet.

We're going to have sex with each other.

I'm excited to see you,
Etgar

I record a video and attach it. In the video I am staring into the computer and I say, "I am not a man. I promise."

I send it.

I'm going to London.

Alice Poem #3
I caught malaria in your dumb canals. I got
a fever and vomited and went the color
of dead daffodils. You said I didn't have malaria.
I have loads of malaria. A+ at having malaria.
I should have been vaccinated, maybe, BUT OH:
if you wake up one day in Uganda it's too
late. I don't know if I'm Cheryl Cole. On TV
Ashley Cole got sent on against Arsenal
and 60,000 people booed him and that is what
I want to happen to you. Please feel like
I feel now.

20

Sitting cross-legged in the center of the living room carpet, I pretend to be a fishing boat lost at sea. I know about what to do if that happens. From the book. I know how to fashion fishing hooks from safety pins. I know about flares. I know about doing an SOS and making solar stills and punching sharks in their noses to scare them away. In *Lost*, when some of them left the island on a boat, they sent up a flare, and evil men came. They stole the boy away and shot someone almost dead. It was ultra-scary.

That's why I am staying away from the Outside.

The television comes on. It's the news. The bald man is here. He shuffles a sheaf of papers and coughs and looks at me. His tie is loose and his collar is foxed with old sweat. The screen behind him shows a photo of the earth, spinning faster than a bike wheel, so that the colors slide into one long smear.

"Good morning," he says. "Someone died today and a hurricane happened. Something else happened and something else happened. The banks did something. A footballer kicked a football referee. Someone had sex with someone else." I tip the glass back until it's vertical and empty. My body is humming. "And, in an unexpected turn of events, Etgar Allison has arranged to meet with Macy Anderson, a thirty-five-year-old Scottish female he has been romantically linked to via the Internet. The trip will be financed with money left to Allison by his late grandmother, who died aged ninety-two at a computer with bingo on the screen." I wonder if everyone is going to start dying at computers now. I wonder what will be open on my computer when I die. Probably the Wikipedia page for death or Netflix or a chat window with someone I will never meet. Probably Alice's photo albums. Probably interracial porn. "The purpose of the trip remains unclear, although it has been suggested that Allison is attempting to gain a sense of perspective and break his recent cycle of self-destructive behavior." That's fucking stupid, I feel. I'm going to London to have sex with Macy because Macy is sexy, and nothing else is happening. Alice is gone. Mum and Dad are away. Aslam is being a dick. I want to be next to someone and nothing else. I don't need perspective. I have perspective. I have good perspective. My perspective is: Alice cheated on me and I broke up with her and I'm sad and everything's scary. I'm also drunk. Heavy weather. "When questioned, he declined to comment and lashed out aggressively in a manner perceived to be 'out of sorts' with his usual character. More soon."

I have a mouthful of Dad's Famous Grouse and go upstairs. I climb into bed and read some of the book. There's nothing in it for this. There are only diagrams showing how to deactivate bombs.

I put it down and fall asleep.

*

"Etgar?" a voice says. "It's me. Get up." I do a rumbling sound and roll over. "Etgar, come on. You look fucked. Wake up." I slap a hand away. Why do people keep waking me up? I don't want to be awake. That's why I'm asleep. "Etgar."

I sit up. It's Aslam. He's come in by vaulting the back fence and walking through the sunroom. It was easy because I left the sunroom open. Usually he comes in through one of its windows. When I'm getting into his place, I go through the living room windows, or through the kitchen skylight, which stays open a lot because their smoke alarm's so sensitive.

"Aslam?" I say. "What the fuck are you doing?" I

kick off the cover and heave myself out. I'm still in the mud-flecked panda suit.

He steps back. "What the fuck have you been doing? Is that Hattie's? What happened to your face?"

"I told you not to come over."

"Are you drunk?"

I push him to one side and go to hold my face under the bathroom tap. He leans in the doorway. Cold water calms my swollen eyes. I let some into my mouth. It feels like the first time. I blink and try to shrug out the straightness in my shoulders.

"Why are you here?"

"Why are you being such a dick? I came to ask if you wanted to come and get drunk and play Monopoly at Amy's. She finally asked me over, but it's with other people."

"Who's Amy?"

"I've told you about her a fuck ton of times. That girl. The girl I've liked the past month."

"Just go."

"I'm not going. You're fucked."

"I'm fine."

"I'm going to call your mum."

"You're not."

I put one hand on the door frame and look past him. I'm trying to make him leave with my eyes. It isn't working. They aren't intimidating eyes.

"What have you been doing?"

"It doesn't matter. Nothing. Go."

"Why are you being a twat?"

"I'm not being a twat. I want to be on my own for a while. Me and Alice broke up. I want to sit on the sofa and eat ice cream and watch films like people do in films."

"It doesn't look like you've been eating ice cream and watching films."

"Well, I have."

"What films did you watch?"

"One with Jews and Nazis and Daniel Craig." I walk downstairs. He follows. In the living room, he picks up an empty bottle of wine and reads the label out loud. He says it how I said it. Cab-er-net Soh-vig-non. I unlock the front door and hold it open. "It's pronounced Cah-bern-ey Soh-vin-yon. Now go, please."

"No. And why are you drinking red wine?"

"I'll call the police."

"Me too."

"What?"

"They're kind. I like them." He sits down in the armchair, leaning back and crossing his arms. "This is an intervention now. You have to stop doing whatever you're doing. Your parents will be back soon."

"I'm not doing anything. I'm sleeping. I'll see you at school."

"Stop being a dick."

"Fuck off."

"It was only Alice. It wasn't like your wife or something. Fuck's sake."

I walk over to where he's sitting and hit him.

I don't know why I've started being able to hit people. I don't know where it's coming from. My body is doing a lot of things without me telling it to, I feel. These don't seem like decisions I would make. I don't know.

It's not a real punch. It lightly connects with his right cheek. But his face changes so quickly it's like it's been replaced with someone else's. And the someone else's eyes have collapsed in the corners and the someone else's lips are wobbling and the someone else's body doesn't know what to do.

He uncrosses his arms and stands up and walks into the Outside. He doesn't close the door or look around. He leaves. I hit him. So he left. Seems reasonable. I hit Aslam. He said "only Alice." He doesn't understand. The longest relationship he had was with Callie Tripton. It lasted for five months and ended when he put it in her butt and she head-butted him.

Not butt.

Ass. Ass. Ass.

I hit him.

Aslam.

In the face.

With my hand.

My actual hand.

The hand that belongs to me.

Amundsen wanders into the living room. He goes to the open door, sniffs the air, and comes back to lie at my feet. I scratch behind his ears with my big toe. He yawns. I get up to close the door and we get back under the duvet.

21

When the sun is mostly gone, I put on Mum's coat and walk to the big supermarket down past the Baptist church and the roundabout. I'm heavy and sick. A streetlight comes on as I walk past. I'm Dumbledore. The trees are anorexic. Their roots wrestle with the pavement and lose, so they tilt at odd angles over cars and those green metal boxes with I don't know what inside them.

The security guard outside Tesco's looks down at me and I look down at me, and we both see the panda legs sticking out of Mum's coat. I nod at him. He doesn't nod back. He's got thick, dark hair but no eyebrows.

The supermarket is busy. My heart goes double-time. Most of the people are young. Young couples with baskets full of wine and pasta. I should get wine and pasta. I should have a romantic meal with Amundsen. We should get drunk and then sleep until we're dragged out of the house by people Mum found on the Internet after Googling *my son will not move*.

I take a basket and move down the aisles slowly, doing my best not to look at anyone above the waist. I pick up ham, chips, a large purple vegetable, a tomato, an apple, eight Polish beers, and a bottle of Captain Morgan's. My arm is coming out of its socket so I do a half-run to the checkouts. While I'm passing the Smirnoff Ice, someone starts calling my name. I usually ignore it when this happens because I'm anxious that the person isn't calling my name, they're calling the name of their friend, who coincidentally is standing nearby. I don't want to look retarded, so I don't answer.

They call my name again.

A hand falls on my shoulder.

I turn around and put my basket on the floor. It's Sarah Clemence, Matt Wilkes, and some other people from school. They've got a trolley filled with Smirnoff Ice, beer, and cocktail sausages. They're smiling and finishing laughs.

"Etgar," Sarah says. "Are you okay? What happened to your face?"

"Nothing. Hi. I fell into a lamppost. Walked into it."

"It looks sore. You should put peas on it. Are you having a party?"

I look down at my basket. "No," I say. "It's for my mum."

"Cool. Some people are up at the woods. Do you want to come? We've got like room in the tents and stuff. And get Aslam. Lots of people are up there."

I tense my hands and feet. "I can't. I've got to help my mum with her party. It's her special party." What's that supposed to mean?

"Aw. Come on. It'll be fun."

"You should come, man," Matt says.

The others are looking at bottles.

"Did you hear about that footballer kicking that football referee?" I say.

"What?"

"Nothing."

"Um. So are you coming?"

"I can't. Thank you. Have fun."

I pick up my basket with both hands and turn around and walk at an inappropriate pace away from them. I feel bad about it. It looks rude. I want to hide. I want to be deep under the ground. I want to be so deep that the heat from the center of the earth melts my skin and bones and I am gone.

The woman who scans my items doesn't look up. She looks at something beyond me and sighs intermittently. I'm grateful. I put the purchase on my card and go to the pharmacy counter near the exit. The woman there is wearing a Lloyds shirt and arranging boxes of generic medicine on a shelf behind the counter. She waves her polka-dot fingernails at me, yawns, and asks how she can help.

"A box of Nytol, please. The 50mg ones." She looks me in the eyes before getting them. She is checking if she can see a suicider or a drug addict in them. She is looking for deep blackness and severe discontent. I try to project domestic calm. "They're for my mum. She's experiencing severe menstrual cramps and isn't sleeping so well." The woman winces and nods. I pay and leave.

*

Macy has replied to my email. She says that the meeting is in central London, so any hotel in Zone 1 will be okay. I go onto my bank's website and transfer the Gran money from my savings account to my current account. Mum won't find out. I'll do sixth form and get a job in Tesco and never tell her. She said I would need it for college. I won't need it for college because I won't go to college. I will marry into extreme wealth. I feel 90 percent sure that I will eventually marry someone I meet on the Internet. I feel 90 percent sure that the person will not be Macy.

I'm in bed, naked, drinking beer and looking at hotel websites. They all look the same. They all look clean and marble and the color of sand. I book one near Marble

Arch. It costs two hundred and seven pounds for one night. That's enough for 207 beers. That's enough for sex with four cheap prostitutes.

She's online.

"I booked a hotel," I say. "Near Marble Arch."

"That sounds great, hon. I can't wait to see you."

"Yeah. Me too."

"I'm vaguely nervous."

"Don't be."

Do be. I'm a child. You are going to feel like a pedophile and run away. We are going to sit on separate toilet floors and cry until we fall asleep.

"I keep thinking about you meeting me off the plane. We instantly recognize each other. We hold each other so tight it hurts and we kiss. I'm already wet."

"That sounds nice."

"Then you lead me into the toilet and you fuck me."

"I fuck you in the toilet."

"For an hour."

"For an hour."

"For two hours."

"Mm."

"Forever."

I stare at my computer screen. I want to cry. I want tears to fly out of my eyes like I'm a character in *Titanic* and I've just lost everyone I love. I want to collapse. I want to sleep for one hundred days and wake up somewhere unfamiliar and empty.

"I can't wait. I'm so horny right now. Might have to have a little play."

"I have to go," I say. "I have a meeting."

"Shame, hon. I'll be thinking of you. Let me know the name of the hotel and give me a time. I can't wait."

"Me neither."

I finish the beer and open another one. I watch a video of a woman killing a kitten by standing on it in stilettos. She punctures its tiny belly and purple bulbs spill out. Splashes of blood throw themselves onto her toes. The kitten yelps for a while then is gone.

There are twenty Nytol in the box. I take ten. I close the door and lie on my back and stare at the ceiling.

22

We were sitting at opposite ends of Alice's bath, under a foot of foam. Morning was coming. We hadn't slept. I planted my foot against her face, trying to fit my big toe into her nostril. Her face folded up into tiny mountain ranges.

"It still doesn't fit," Alice said.

"It will," I said. "I read yesterday that your ears and nose are the only things that never stop growing. It's the cartilage or something. Because they're made of that."

"We'll be like eighty and then you'll fit your toe in my nose."

"Yeah."

23

There are gray moths and spiders play-fighting on the ceiling. I know they aren't there, but I can see them. They aren't so scary. Watching them is watching an open tap. It is slow and predictable and okay. I could watch them for a long time. I will keep watching. Look up. They walk on straight tracks and sporadically shiver in unison.

I'll play helicopter on the computer.

Crash.

Crash.

Points.

Crash.

This is hard.

Everything is hard.

There is no water left in my mouth. I should go and get a glass of water. I'll do that. I'm in the kitchen. I don't know why I'm in the kitchen. Touch things. Try to remember. It was probably food. Put pizza in the microwave. It won't fit. Okay, calzone. They left a lot of frozen food. Maybe I should cook more of it. I'm in the toilet now. Lying in the bath now. It's empty. It's dark here. Slow death party forever. The sink is full of gold-fish. Spiders. I want to see a whale. I should call Alice and make her come. Ask her to bring a whale. No, I wouldn't do that. Because of something. Is it too late in life to start ballet? I remember Billy Elliot. He jumped and clicked his heels. Thirsty. I'll play helicopter on the computer.

Crash.

Crash.

Aslam in my bedroom. Breaking in again. Hi. Thirsty. Aslam, can I have water? No, I haven't seen that yet. It sounds good. I'll watch it. I watched that other one. The stabbing one. There was sex and then dying. When she died she didn't cry. I kept thinking, *Cry.* I kept wanting to reassure her. Do you ever want to climb inside the TV? To get goals or be somewhere warmer? No, I haven't seen that either. Is that Eminem? Brittany Murphy died. I don't know how. Someone said it somewhere. She had sex with Eminem in the metal factory. She died. We should make films. I know you always say it. We should make a film where we sail a ship to an island filled with sexy women and we marry the women and throw rocks at the moon. No, we ride whales. No, we dig tunnels under the ground and live in them. We blow up houses from underneath. We blow up big Tesco. Mums die.

Aslam, you've gone.

Okay.

Where are you?

This is not funny.

Really want to ride a whale. I don't know where Aslam's gone. Thirsty. Whale. Go and get water. I'm in the garden. There was something here. I came here for something. What. What. What if I hit my head for long enough, will the memories surface? Like bubbles. Forehead in the grass. Bubbles. What did I want here? Water. I want water. That's the toilet. No, kitchen. Let's go. Army. I don't want to be here. It's cold. Antarctica. Amundsen. Where is Amundsen? I know you can hear me. Let's kiss. You taste like purple meat and grass and burnt rubber. Join the army with me. Let's go somewhere. Let's be comets.

The doorbell. Answer it. Walk. Legs. I'm in the kitchen. I'm in my bedroom. I'm in the kitchen. What is happening? The doorbell is shouting. That is what is happening. Okay. Answer. I want a drink of water. Open the door. Oh. It's Alice. Come in. Hi. Thanks. I missed you. You came from Antigua. Yes, I'm okay. Your cheeks are bright. Your skin has eaten sun. Water. Wait, what. I'm on the stairs. Where's Alice. Alice? ALICE. You left.

The door's open. You went outside. ALICE. It's night-time. You'll get stabbed. Come back. ALICE. Oh God. You'll die. You'll get taken.

Crash.

ALICE.

Go outside. Find Alice. Alice. Alice. It's cold out here tonight. Everything carries on forever in every direction. A man. Ask him. ALICE. Have you seen Alice? He's running away. Come back. Help. ALICE. Alice is gone. Please. Where is she? Did you see her? It's cold out here. Alice. Oh. ALICE.

24

"Oh my God," Alice said. "Look how dead she is." We were standing over her mum's open casket.

"Pretty dead," I said.

Alice reached down to prod her mum's cheek.

"Jesus," she said. "What are we supposed to do?"

PART 3

Simultaneous

25

Sometimes I think of atoms as tiny people who are extremely scared and hold hands with each other a lot. I imagine that my body is made of tiny, scared people, and they pick up mugs and books that are made of other tiny, scared people. And when you sex someone it's just lots of tiny, scared people holding hands.

I think about the tiny people that are me and I feel less alone.

I'm an army of tiny people, trying their best.

They work in a tall building (my body). They have meetings and parties and office romances. When I vomit, that's people getting fired. When I eat, I'm hiring. When I'm dizzy, it's a fire drill. When I die, the tiny people will wander off and look for new jobs. As plants and dirt and people. Some of the tiny people (my bones) will stay for a long time, not wanting to admit that everything is over.

That's what I'm thinking about now, naked, with my head inside the toilet. Regurgitated noodles are stacking up in small underwater pyramids. All of the muscles in my face are being stretched like elastic bands, and I can't breathe and I can't feel anything, which feels good.

When I'm empty, I feel better. I lie on the bathroom floor and hum. It's eight and my train leaves at twelve. My body's still asleep. There are children on my shoulders, swinging their legs against my shoulder blades. Amundsen pads up to the open bathroom door and cocks his head. There's heavy weather in his eyes. We haven't been going for walks. He misses the Outside. He doesn't get anxious, because we never hit him. Not even when he shat in Mum's shoes and she put her feet in them. Not even when he jumped up to hug an old woman and she fell over asleep or unconscious. He doesn't know what being hit is.

"Okay," I say, convulsing as another length of bile abseils from my mouth. I am indifferent to my existence now. My existence is like India. My existence is like a basking shark in the middle of the Atlantic. It isn't connected to me anymore. It isn't a fact of me. It is just here, next to me, like a lamp or a microwave.

*

It's balmy and mild outside. Mabel is dragging herself past the far trees with Mushroom. I wave. She smiles. There's something in my eyes that lets her know I don't want to talk. We watch the dogs kiss each other's bums. She tells me about being a dancer for a harmonica band when she was young. She tells me about rationing. She tells me about dancing dances I don't know with people who are now dead.

*

I try to get into my funeral suit, but it's too small. It's from when I was thirteen. From when Alice's mum died from the wars that were happening in her breasts. The funeral happened in the church on Emery Lane. It was the first time any of us had been inside. We took ketamine and Alice kept whispering that she felt as if she went on forever as the coffin got carried in and put down. She fell asleep behind a quiz machine at the wake. Her dad stood on a table for his speech. It's the only thing I remember clearly.

"Death is just something that happens to people, but it is the worst fucking thing that happens to people, and it's going to happen to everyone." He started pointing. "To you and you and you, Brenda, to you, Brian, actually you're probably next." Alice's uncles pulled him down by the elbows and dropped him onto a bench. The room applauded and someone did a cheers.

We stayed in bed a lot that year. We stayed in bed so long I started to think our bodies were taking on the shape of cellos. We watched documentaries about faraway places and looked up ticket prices to them, knowing we could never go.

I put on Dad's funeral suit instead. I drink. He's not a big person, but he's bigger than I am.

*

I get a taxi to the station, because I might as well spend everything because what else. The taxi driver asks how I am, and I say I'm really great. He asks where I'm going, and I say London, to meet a woman from the Internet, who I've developed unfamiliar feelings for. He says that he met his second wife on the Internet. He says she used pictures of herself that were ten years old.

On the train, I sit next to a man with large headphones and a duffel coat. He has the window seat. He's asleep. When we start moving, he opens his eyes and unfolds his hands and looks down at them. Maybe he's looking for mouths too. I think about making him this offer: let's both tell each other exactly what to do, from now until it's over. Every time I don't know what to do I'll call Sleeping Man and he'll tell me. *Tell her to get fucked. Choose the lasagna. Wear blue.* Same with him. We will never be confused again. We will be each other's robots.

The station gets eaten by terraced houses, and the terraced houses get eaten by fields that are blank at first then studded with sheep. People take off their coats and turn on their computers and a collective sigh happens. A woman across the aisle opens a packet of cheese and onion chips. She blinks and knocks five into her mouth. They shatter and sound like radio static.

The only thing I brought to read is the book Dad gave me, so I open it at random and try to learn about batting off a bear. I learn about how to give someone a tracheotomy with a ballpoint pen. You just cut a hole, put it in, and blow. Welcome back to life. I hope it gets better.

*

When the refreshment cart pulls up, I think about asking for one of everything, like Harry Potter in the first book. I could share all of the food with Sleeping Man and we could get drunk and form unbreakable bonds through the shared feeling of being a deforested forest.

I don't ask for one of everything.

I ask for peanuts and two cans of premixed Smirnoff and Coke. They cost £4 each. I say "four pounds" out loud while trying to do a smile at Sleeping Man. It doesn't work. I look retarded. Doing smiles is hard. Sleeping Man wakes up and asks for a chicken sandwich, two Twix, and a Magners.

"How much?" he says.

"Nine eighty-five," the woman says.

"Nine eighty-five," I say. "Sweet Mary, Jesus, and someone else." He catches me with his eyes. They have being-tired bruises under them. I think about hugging him. People like hugs. I think everyone wants to be hugged at all times, but everyone is scared so no one does. Everyone has to sit around being unhugged. There should be people who are paid by the government to sit on public transport hugging people. The people should be called Hugabees.

Head Hugabee.

Hugabee of the Year.

Hugabee Headquarters.

No, that's retarded. Everyone would sue the Hugabees, and they'd get upset and disappear.

I eat the peanuts and drink one of the vodkas. There is a high-pitched female voice leaking from Sleeping Man's headphones. He puts the sandwich onto his plastic table and goes back to sleep. The woman in front of us answers a call. She's excitedly making plans to walk the length of whatever river runs between London and Manchester. She is talking about verdant landscapes and kind weather. She says the word *contemplation*.

I want to be excited.

I want to walk along rivers.

Wait, I don't. That's boring. I don't want to contemplate anything. I want to want something instead of not wanting things all the time. I want to get drunk. I finish the vodkas, get up, and walk to the buffet car. I buy a miniature Heineken and another Smirnoff and Coke. I drink them quickly in my seat, close my eyes, and think, *See you in London.*

26

"So do her tits fall off?" Aslam said. "Like with the hair?" He sank a hand into his bucket of popcorn and leaned back. An advert for a film about talking warrior owls was playing on the big screen. We were fourteen.

"No, you twat," Sam said. "They cut them off. It's called a mastectomy."

"They actually cut off the tits?"

"Yeah," Alice said. She was holding an Evian bottle half-filled with vodka and Coke. It was the first day of the Christmas holidays, and we'd taken her to see *50/50* because of it having Seth Rogen in it and being about not dying from cancer. "She says they'll cut them off and then give her fake plastic ones to stick on so no one will be able to tell."

"Etgar would love that job."

"What job?"

"Cutting off tits."

"Fuck off."

"Excuse me," someone said. We all turned in our seats. A man whose hair made the shape of a toilet seat was leaning forward. He was wearing glasses but looking over the top of them, and he was holding a Styrofoam coffee cup and he was tall. The woman next to him was wide. Her lips were the color of pomegranates. "Would you mind keeping it down?"

"Sorry," I said. "We'll be quiet."

"It's the fucking adverts," Aslam said. I punched him in the shoulder.

"Sorry," I said again. We turned back to face the screen. A small boy was wandering around New York while inspiring music played. A voiceover said things about life and love and death.

"Right," Aslam said. "So do they cut off the whole of the tit or like just the nipple?"

"You retard," Sam said. "Why would someone just have cancer in the nipple?"

"I don't know. Why would someone just have cancer in the tits?"

"She might not just have cancer in the tits. We don't know yet. The cancer might have gone to other bits."

"What does that mean?"

"It means she might die."

"No," I said.

"Excuse me," the man with toilet-seat-shaped hair said. We turned around again. The wide woman had crossed her arms. "I asked nicely, now could you please keep it down? The film's going to start in a second."

"Her mum's got cancer," Aslam said, pointing at Alice.

"Cancer," Sam said, nodding.

"Of the tits."

"I'm very sorry to hear that," the man said. "But I'd still like to watch the film."

"I'd like to watch the film too," Aslam said. "That's why I'm here. Only the film hasn't started yet. So don't shit yourself, gaylord."

"Would you like me to call someone?"

"Yeah, call your mum and tell her she's a twat."

I groaned and hit Aslam around the back of the head.

"You nasty little prick," the man said, taking hold of Aslam's hood and standing up. I looked at Sam and Sam smiled. He pulled the lid off his large Sprite and nodded at me and threw it over the man.

The man froze.

He didn't know what had happened.

He dropped Aslam and touched his cheek and looked at his hand like it was covered in blood. His wet fringe was pinned against his forehead in thin, gray strands. Everyone started to struggle out down the row of people.

"I'm really sorry," I said, bringing a corner of my shirt up to the man's face. I was thinking about him being on a first date with the wide woman, whom he would maybe fall in love with and marry and visit in the hospital when she was about to die from multiple heart attacks.

"Off," he said. "Fuck. Off."

So I ran after the others. Alice was waiting for me in the aisle. We held hands and left. Two weeks later, Alice's mum died and we all went to the park and Alice drank until she fell asleep and we carried her home.

27

At the hotel reception desk, I hide four open wounds on my left hand. That happens sometimes. I scratch. I took the train from Victoria to Marble Arch, and it was easy. We go with school sometimes. It's hard. I get anxious imagining my cartoon-flat body being peeled off the rails.

The hotel is as shiny as the photographs. It doesn't feel like a place that's been built by humans. It's too big. It feels like a landscape people happen to be passing over.

I say my name and the receptionist gives me a key card. She says something about breakfast. Each of her hands is half the width of mine. I expect her to stop me. I expect her to tell me that children aren't allowed in hotel rooms. I expect her to accuse me of credit card fraud and do a citizen's arrest on me.

She doesn't.

She smiles.

I walk quickly across the marble foyer to an elevator. Floor four. The elevator door opens and a blonde woman pushes out an elderly man in a wheelchair. The man is asleep. Orange cubes of food are nestled in his beard.

In the room (421), I hold my hand under the tap and dab it with soap. It stings. My heart is going triple-time, but slowing. Everything is soft in the room. Everything is the color of biscuits. I lie on the bed and boil the mini-kettle for tea. I fall asleep and dream about having underwater sex with a mermaid Macy. The sun gets too close and the water evaporates and she dies. When I wake up, I don't want to move.

*

I'm waiting for Macy in the foyer. We did texts. I said I couldn't meet her at the station because of work. I said I was wearing a somber-looking suit that's outgrown me, and she said she was wearing a gray pencil skirt with a black hoodie. There are more people now, shifting across the marble in pairs with luggage on wheels. It makes me think of ducks. I imagine throwing bread crusts at them. I imagine throwing whole loaves of bread at their heads and then apologizing profusely while staring at the dents in my shoes.

She appears.

She's wearing what she said she was wearing. She seems to have no luggage. Her calves are narrow and tightly curved. Two swaths of blonde hair are pulled back across her forehead and pinned behind her head. She's sexy. She would probably be beautiful if *beautiful* was a word that ever happened in my head.

She puts down her bag and slowly looks around. She pushes a knuckle into the corner of her eye, pulls it away and stares at it. A passing man nods and smiles at her. I think, *Back off.* I walk toward her. She's looking away. I'm very close. Too close, maybe. I take two steps back.

"Macy."

Macy spins.

"Etgar."

We look at each other's faces. There's nothing I recognize in hers. I thought there would be heavy weather. I thought there would be severe disappointment or quiet anger or general upset. None of those are there. Nothing else is, either. Her face is a book written in kanji. There are oil spills under her eyes and brackets around her mouth. I am one pint taller than she is.

I try to make my spine straight and my forearms tense. It is extremely important to try and make myself look like a man. It won't work. I don't know. She will decide now what happens next. She could say nothing and leave the hotel and continue her life minus my interference. I don't know what will help her decision. Something tiny, I feel. Something tiny will tip her scales and drag her away. The size of my feet or the bruises on my face or the spot next to my left nostril.

Everything is just stuff touching other stuff.

There's a hand on my hand. It's Macy's. I was scratching at the open holes. I didn't notice. A line of blood has run down the valley between two of my knuckles. She guides my hand into the pouch of her hoodie and wipes it clean. She is doing a mum smile to me. She is doing a *You are not okay, and I'm sorry* smile.

I don't want to say anything.

I don't want to have to say anything.

I want to stand, unmoving, with my hand in Macy's pouch while she smiles at me like someone who would not kind of have sex with Aaron Mathews and lie about it afterward.

"Thanks," I say. "Sorry. I didn't notice. That happens sometimes. It's . . . I don't know. Sorry. Thank you."

"It's okay, hon. Don't worry. Shall we go up to the room before dinner? I'd like a shower."

"Yes," I say. "Go to groom." I pinch myself. "The room. Okay."

We go to wait in front of the elevator. I catch sight of the receptionist and see that she's been watching. When she sees me seeing her, she quickly finds something more interesting between her hands. I feel braver standing next to someone, neither of us being familiar to anyone else here but each other. I don't know if we are familiar to each other. I know I'm not a mortgage broker. I don't know what Macy is. She's nice. She's here. We both are.

In the elevator, I say, "Aren't you going to leave?"

"Why?"

"I don't know. I'm short."

"You're taller than I am," she says.

*

Macy showers while I use the mini-kettle to make tea. Hearing the water makes me not able not to imagine her naked. She isn't what I expected. I don't know what I expected. I expected a cold, sex-crazed woman who drank coffees I couldn't pronounce and understood quantitative easing. Maybe she is that. She doesn't seem like that. We went into the elevator and along the corridor. I don't understand why she is here. I don't understand why she hasn't disappeared.

I put two teabags in two mugs and add water. There's only Earl Grey. Earl Grey tastes like ugly flowers. I turn on the television. The bald man's there. I don't want to listen to him. I don't want to think. I take a small bottle of pink wine out of the minibar and drink it under the duvet, reading about fighting alligators in *The Worst-Case Scenario Survival Handbook.*

When Macy comes out of the bathroom, she's wearing a black dress that makes her look like a woman from a James Bond film. Her hair is half-dry. It has all been flipped onto one side of her head. I feel like an ant lost in a living room carpet.

"What are you reading?" she says, dropping onto a corner of the bed and tugging a brush through her hair.

"Nothing," I say. "A book about not dying."

She laughs. "I like Martina Cole."

"Me too," I say. "No. I don't know what that is."

"Are you ready for dinner?"

"Okay."

*

Everything feels different when we sit down in the hotel restaurant. The other people are in matching pairs. Wearing their own clothes. Talking about holidays. Drinking after-dinner espressos. Serious people doing serious lives. We are two people who sexed on the Internet. Macy could be my mum. What if I'm adopted and she is my mum? That's happened before. Not to me. It was on the news.

A waiter comes over and asks if we'd like wine. I nod. I point at two words in the middle of the list. I have decided not to try and pronounce anything ever again. The waiter disappears. Me and Macy hide behind our menus.

Choosing food in restaurants is difficult. I always want to split into several people and eat various meals, then vomit everything back up and become one person again, to choose my favorite.

Macy chooses quickly. She folds her menu up and leans back, picking at the fabric of her dress like a scab.

The waiter comes back, holding the wine in a retarded clawlike way. He pours a very small amount into my glass. I look at him, confused.

"Could I have some more?"

"Don't you want to try it?" He nods at the glass.

I nod at him.

He nods again. "It might be terrible," he says, winking.

I think, *Yes, it will definitely be terrible, because it's wine.* I don't understand. I pick up the glass and pour some into my mouth. I try not to wince. The waiter stares at me. I stare at the waiter.

"Is it okay?"

"Um. Yes."

"Good."

He pours more wine into my glass, then leans over to fill up Macy's. She's biting her lip to keep a laugh from coming out. I don't understand. I don't understand why I had to try it. Nothing would happen if I didn't like it. No one likes the taste of wine.

The bottle lands on the table between us. We tell the waiter what we want. I choose risotto. Macy chooses steak. Our menus disappear with the waiter and there's nothing left to hide behind, except the wine glasses, which are almost windows.

I try to think of things to say. I run through films in

my head, searching for relevant quotes. *Wine,* I think. *Sideways.*

I take a sip from my glass. "It tastes like the back of a fucking L.A. schoolbus," I say. It comes out louder than I expected and in a voice that isn't mine. I wince. "Sorry," I say. "No, it doesn't."

Macy stares at me, curiously and kindly, and with her mouth open. Other people stare at me too.

We use a lot of nothing words to fill up the space between us. I ask how she is. She says okay. She asks how I am. I say fine. I ask how her trip was. She says okay. She asks if I've been here before. I say no. It's like the talking you do with teachers when you see them outside of school. When you know you have to say something but you don't know what you have to say. We both sit up straight and take big glugs of wine. There are a lot of elephants on the table. They are miniature and pink and we aren't yet sure what shape they are. I try to work out how much each glug of wine is costing. Fifty pence, I think.

When we're more drunk and familiar, talking gets less weird. The waiter brings our food. Neither of us eats. I try to ask Macy about her business, but she doesn't want to talk about it. She asks about mortgage brokering.

"Never mix work and food and women, I always say," I say. I don't always say that. And it doesn't sound very suave. "More wine?" *Suave* is a very suave word.

"Thanks."

I use the retarded claw way of holding the wine while I pour it. I pour some into mine, and start pouring some into Macy's. I drop the wine bottle on her steak. It sits there, flowing off the table and into the deep green sea of carpet. Macy laughs very loudly. People look at us. The waiter sees and walks over. He picks up the wine and Macy's plate.

"I'm terribly sorry," he says.

"Why?" I say.

Macy starts laughing again. I nudge her foot with my foot and hoist up my eyebrows. It means *This is funny, but let's pretend to be serious for the waiter because he's a normal human man trying to do his normal human job.* She coughs.

"That's fine," she says. "Another bottle of the same and another steak would be super."

He leaves. I pour half of my wine into her glass. She finishes it in one sip. She quietly says "Jesus," and she's smiling. I think, *I'm not doing a good job of not looking like a child.* I finish my wine.

"Do you go on a lot of dates?"

She knows.

"Yes," I say. "I mean no. Some. Sometimes. The bottle was very slippery. I think he dipped it in water. I'll ask him not to do that again." I turn around to look for the waiter. I say, "Waiter."

"You're very tense."

"Sorry."

"Don't be sorry."

"Okay."

I put my finger in my risotto, then take it out. It's supposed to make me look comfortable and at ease. It doesn't work. I look brain damaged and overly tactile.

"Are you always anxious around people?"

"Only around byoofell lades," I say. "Oh God." I put a hand over my face and open a *V* between my fingers to see through. "Beautiful loodies," I say. "Fuck." Macy is laughing again. I can count her teeth through the gap in my hand. "Beautiful ladies," I say. "There." She reaches forward and pulls my hand away. Her hand is cold. It is a good, gentle cold, like drinking water in the bath.

"Come out." More wine and another steak arrive. My glass fills up. "Can you show him how to pour?" Macy says. The waiter sets the bottle down on the table and demonstrates the claw. I make one with my hand. He picks up the bottle and lodges it between my thumb and fingers. Shaking slightly, I pour my own wine. To the brim.

"Very good," he says. "Only usually we do a little less."

"Thanks."

"It's hard," I say, turning to Macy as the waiter leaves. "I keep thinking it will come out of my hand and smash into a thousand pieces and I'll fall into the pieces. Then doctors will have to graft skin from my bum onto my face."

"I'll lend you skin."

"I'll look nicer."

"It'll be like you're wearing plastic bags."

"No," I say.

We start on our food. Mine is cold and tastes of old cheese and paper. Macy's smells good. I can't eat steak because it makes my mouth too tired. Risotto is easy. Risotto is baby food. I drink wine every two mouthfuls, and it starts to taste less bad. I think, maybe acquired taste is actually a real thing. Maybe people do like wine. It's not as nice as just eating the grapes, but it's okay. And it makes me less anxious. My shoulders start to sag, and rush hour in my head comes to a close. The bears get home to their wives and go to bed. Night-night, everyone.

"That was good," Macy says.

"You have some on your mouth."

She dabs at her lips.

"Is it gone?"

"No. It's sort of on your cheek. Left."

She dabs at her cheek.

"Now?"

"No."

"Can you get it?"

"Okay."

She hands me the napkin and leans across the table. I drop it. I jab my finger into her nostril. She yelps and pulls away. I push Dad's tie into my mouth. I realize I am drunk. The nose thing was what I used to do to Alice, when we weren't in the bath and I couldn't do it with my toe.

"That felt weird."

"You have an empty nose. It's clean. Well done."

"Thanks, hon."

"Sorry for putting my finger in your nose."

"Forgiven."

"Do you want dessert?"

"Dessert wine?"

"Deal."

Macy waves the waiter over and we order more wine. I'm starting to get tingles. My body is always drunk before my head. When bad things happen from drinking, the last memory I usually have is realizing that my body feels heavy and warm.

28

Me and Macy are holding hands in the back of a black cab. Outside, the sky is black and glassy. Our driver isn't saying anything. He's got the radio on low, and it's playing something depressing by Adele. I wonder who he thinks we are. We look like a middle-class mum and son, I feel.

Macy asked him to drive us to the closest gay nightclub. It wasn't my idea, and I don't know why it's happening. I'm drunk. We didn't have sex. We finished the wine, then had mojitos because I said I didn't know what they were, and I still don't know what they are and I definitely don't like them.

"Are you sure it's gay?" Macy says. She releases my hand. We pull up beside a converted warehouse with a neon purple entrance. There's a line running past a fenced-off area where people are smoking and kissing and touching hands.

The driver laughs. "Gay," he says. I push money through the window that separates us, and Macy and I climb out. We join the back of the line, behind a man with bleached hair and scuffed boots. Macy takes my hand again. A thick, heavy thud is coming from inside the building.

Nightclubs are scary.

There are too many people having fun in ways I don't understand. It doesn't make sense. Once, me, Alice, and Aslam got into Diva with fake IDs. People were shouting and hitting each other in the face. A man asked me something and I didn't hear properly, so I didn't reply. I smiled a little. The man said "Fucking retard" to his friend. I smiled more. One of the men pushed me. I pulled my T-shirt up over my head and sat down on the sugar-wet wooden floor. Alice hooked her hands under my armpits, pulled me up, and led me outside. We caught the 84 back to her house. We watched four episodes of *Parks and Recreation*, then fell asleep in our clothes.

We're at the front of the queue. A tall man in a bomber jacket looks at the face on my pretend driver's license. His lip twitches. I look like a gerbil in the picture. Macy doesn't get asked for ID. She reaches for her pocket but stops midway, examines her knuckles, and looks directly up. I put my debit card into a reader, and someone stamps black balloons onto our wrists and we go inside.

"This is going to be fun," Macy says.

"What?"

"This is going to be fun."

"Oh."

People aren't fun.

There are a thousand bears wrestling under revolving lights and lasers. Several men are topless. Layers of sweat cover their chests like cellophane. My body accumulates weight. I am as heavy as one hundred hotel rooms. I try to dig through the floors of my pockets. Maybe I can escape. I will make tiny tunnels and disappear down them. No. Breathe. Stay here with Macy. Then have sex with her. That's why you're here. Look:

Her hips are scales and her fingers are against the back of my neck. I should try to dance. I should try to make my body move in an appealing way. I should seduce her with my body-popping prowess. Macy is Shakira. I will be Ricky Martin.

Left.

Right.

Left.

Jesus.

I look severely retarded. If I keep doing this someone is going to make me sit in a wheelchair. Someone is going to call an ambulance. Are people looking? It's hard to see anything. The lights are blue now. We're in a loud underwater cave. Macy's grinning. Her eyes are closed. I don't understand. We have been inside for one minute.

I want to be not inside for all of the minutes left between now and forever.

"I'll get drinks," I say.

"What?"

"Drinks."

"What?"

I panic and walk away toward the bar. I tuck in my elbows. There are bears on either side of me. They are holding notes in their fists and leaning forward at uncomfortable angles. Macy's arm curls around my back. Her mouth comes to my ear.

"Are you okay?" she says.

"Yes."

"You don't look okay, hon."

I don't want to be here, but Macy does. I should be able to stand in a building with people and not collapse. I'll drink. I'll drink and learn dancing with my eyes. I've seen *Step Up*. I can try. "I'm okay." I'm Channing Tatum.

Macy orders our drinks. She gets two half-orange, half-red cocktails that come in glasses shaped like fruit bowls.

"Relax," she shouts.

"I am relaxed," I shout.

"Good."

"Yeah."

I hold the fruit bowl in both hands and tip whatever the liquid is back into my mouth. Trickles of orange escape my cheeks and drip off my chin. Macy laughs.

She passes me hers and I drink that too. My stomach mumbles. Warmth spreads through my canals.

"Come on," Macy says. I follow her through the tight spaces between bodies. Gaps open and close like elevator doors. I think, *This doesn't make sense.* My legs keep moving. I am relying on my legs not to get too upset and lie down. I ricochet off wet shoulders. Macy stops in a small clearing, raises her hands over her head, and begins to rotate her hips. I want to run forward and hug her. I want to bury my head between her breasts and disappear. I can't. I have to try.

*

I'm trying to make my body bend while Rihanna sings about love and how it goes away. There are more people now. My phone starts to ring. It's Hattie. I want to answer it. I try to push out a path to somewhere quieter.

"CAN YOU HEAR ME?" she says.

"YES."

"ETGAR?"

"YES." I find a corner to press myself into, next to the women's toilet.

"I THOUGHT I LOVED YOU BUT IT WAS JUST BECAUSE JAMES WAS SO FAMILIAR AND YOU AREN'T AND I DON'T KNOW BUT I DEFINITELY DON'T AND WE SHOULD STOP DOING THE

HUMPING BECAUSE I'M GOING TO BE SERIOUS WITH JAMES FROM NOW ON."

I didn't expect her to call and say that. I didn't expect her to call. I'm happy she did.

"Okay."

"OKAY?"

"OKAY."

"OKAY."

"I'M SORRY FOR BEING A DICK I WASN'T GOOD AT THINKING ABOUT OTHER PEOPLE THIS WEEK."

"I'M SORRY TOO. HAVE FUN WHEREVER YOU ARE. SEE YOU ON TUESDAY."

I feel a little lighter. I'm going to go and pick Macy up. I'm going to ask her to teach me dancing. I'm going to be fine.

*

She's gone. She disappeared. I don't know when. I don't know what's happening. A woman came wearing holsters filled with Jägermeister and sold me three shots. Then I danced more. Then a song came on and all the arms went up and I was looking through the arms for Macy's, and they weren't there.

I'm standing at the bar. I'm holding a bottle of lime-flavor Mexican beer, trying to make my breathing get slow. I imagine my lungs as an accordion playing the funeral march. I close my eyes and see Alice behind them. She's sitting at the opposite end of the bath, with panda eyes, shaking her head. I think, *Fuck you. You had fun being fingered by Aaron Mathews. I'm going to have fun in a gay nightclub in London. I'm going to finger the fuck out of everyone. I'm going to forget that you exist. I'm going to drown you.*

"Can I get you a drink?" a man next to me says. He's around Macy's age and wearing a denim jacket above loose blue chinos. His hair is parted in the middle, each side tucked behind an ear. I want to run away, but I'm going to have fun. I'm going to have so much fun.

"Yes," I say, pointing out a random yellow bottle on the glass shelf over the bartender's head. The man next to me does a *come here, now, it's your job* gesture with his hand. He orders the drinks, drops a forearm onto the bar, and leans to one side. I pinch at thigh skin through my pocket. "Alan," the man says, picking my hand up from my side and shaking it.

"Wicked," I say. "Super doop."

"Now you tell me yours."

"Oscar." Alan lets go of my hand. He's been holding it for an unusually long amount of time. I think, *Does Alan fancy me?* I think, *Probably not. He just wants someone to stand with. That's all anyone wants. We'll both stand here. Macy will come back. It's okay. Breathe.*

Have fun.

Alan downs his drink and tells me to do the same. I

do the same. He leads me away from the bar and starts to dance gently against my side. I close my eyes. I make my arms take turns up and down. I picture a team of narwhals congregated in a morning sea, trying to get close and not being able to. Alan grunts. His head's moving like a cartoon Egyptian. I don't want him to be upset but also I don't want him to grind me. He puts a hand against my back. The muscles in my legs involuntarily tense so hard it hurts.

Have fun.

Katy Perry's playing. Alan mouths the words at me. He's grinning and his eyebrows are almost lost in his hair. I try to make my eyes go blank and bright.

"Baby, you're a firework."

What does that even mean? There are better metaphors to flatter people with, I feel. Alice and I played metaphors in the mornings sometimes. "You are an infinite Jacuzzi." "You are a vat of Nesquik tea." "You are afternoon naps."

She's back.

She won't leave.

Go away. You don't live here anymore. I'll call the police.

Have fun.

Alan has a boner now. He isn't trying to conceal it. It's nudging my leg like Amundsen when he wants to be stroked. I don't want to stroke you, Alan. I'm sorry. I don't know what to do. There was nothing in the book for this. I only know what to do if he tries to attack me. I know about gouging eyes and head-butting noses and kneeing balls. I don't know about how to stop a smiling man from grinding me. He looks happy. He looks content.

Have fun.

Alan spins me.

I think, *What is fun and how do you tell when you are having it?* This doesn't feel like fun. Maybe I don't understand fun. Maybe this is exactly what fun is and I don't like fun, but that's okay because I do like some things:

– Masturbating as soon as you wake up. Sometimes over things from your dreams or vintage porns or Rashida Jones.

– Whistling to the theme tune for *CSI: New York* in bed when it's late.

– Yogurt.

– Rum.

– Macy.

– I don't know.

but not this. Definitely not this.

"Sorry," I say. "I need to go."

"Wait," Alan says.

"Bye."

"I bought you a drink."

"Sorry." He seizes me by the arms. I see a bear the size of an apartment block, with fat yellow teeth connected by webs of saliva and eyes like glasses of red wine. He is going to swallow me. I'm going to starve to death inside the cathedral of his stomach. My tiny people will marry his tiny people. We will all melt into the ground. "No," I say. "Please."

I feel stubble against my cheek. I shout. Alan's lips are on my philtrum. He is kissing me. I should hit him. I should stop hitting people. Hitting people is a counterproductive hobby, I feel. I don't know what to do. Sleeping Man should appear and be my captain. We had a deal. Come on. Appear.

Alan flies away from me. His parted hair sinks until it's planted on the floor. Two men are standing over him. One of the men takes hold of his collar and whispers into his ear and pushes him toward the exit. I feel heavy. He disappears. I know he won't appear again, and it's okay.

Have fun.

I'm sitting on the floor. I didn't realize. Hands grip my armpits. I think about Alice. She's here. She's not. It's the men. They carry me. They carry me through the shoulder gaps, and the air is cool and my back's against a cold brick wall. A cigarette is nudged into my mouth.

"Thanks," I say. I blink and look up. One of the anti-Alan men is holding a lighter. His eyes are soft. He brushes his hair backward. The sky behind his head has gone dark violet. We are in the smoking pen.

"Are you okay?"

"I think so," I say. "Thanks." I scratch my head. "I feel drunk."

They laugh. "You're not gay, are you?" the other man asks. He's wearing small, circular glasses and a teal Ralph Lauren shirt.

"I don't think so."

They laugh again and sit down on the asphalt in front of me. We are a triangle. Their names are Alex and Pablo. They ask who I'm here with and I say, Macy and they want to know about her. I tell them about the Internet. I talk about Alice. I don't know why. They laugh when I say I called her a walrus. They tell me to be nicer to Amundsen because it's unlikely that he'll ever be fingered by Aaron Mathews.

Alex and Pablo have been together for three years. They met because Alex saw Pablo's picture in a fashion magazine and emailed him. Pablo is a model and Alex writes newspaper headlines. Sometimes they read *Twilight* to each other and laugh until they fall asleep.

"You should write a letter," Alex says. "I did that with my last boyfriend. It forces you to slow down and organize everything in your head."

"I'll try it, thanks."

"Don't send it."

"Listen," Pablo says, jumping up. I listen. A familiar piano melody is floating out of the open doors. I stand up. It's Vanessa Carlton. We go back inside. The room is loud with the traffic of voices. People are locked together, singing into each other's mouths, wetly and inaccurately, and happily, like sea lions.

Alex puts me on his shoulders and I knot my arms around his neck. We sway. I shout the words, sometimes falling behind or ahead. I'm burning bright. I feel tall. I look down into bald islands on people's heads. Alex is a concrete ballast. He won't drop me. Maybe I'm gay. No, I already tried that. I'm okay, though. Not everyone is trying to kill me. Maybe I'll forget tomorrow. Maybe I can move in with Alex and Pablo. When we go into the Outside, they'll fight bears off with scooters and unempty threats.

The bridge happens.

Piano again.

Making my way downtown,

walking fast,

faces pass,

and I'm homebound.

I sat in a bush opposite Alice's house and listened to this song twenty-six times once. There were two boys and a moped between me and her front door. They were showing each other pictures of their girlfriends naked. "What the fuck is wrong with her nipples?" one said. "They look like blueberry muffins." "Fuck you," the other one said. "Kailey's cunt's like a BLT." I started laughing. The boys saw me. I threw myself out of the bush and ran until my legs felt like bricks. Alice laughed when I told her. She said they were her brother's friends and that they were nice, just occasionally disgusting.

Vanessa finishes.

Alex sets me back down on my feet. Macy is a few meters away, watching us with her hands on her hips. She's smiling. We kiss. I introduce her to Alex and Pablo. I tickle her hand. I go to the bar and order four bottles of champagne. The bartender asks me if I'm sure.

"Sure as I'll ever be," I say. I have no idea why I say that. I'm not sure if it's even a real saying. It doesn't matter. I cover the numbers on the card machine while I enter my pin. We cheers with the champagne bottles. We cheers to Vanessa Carlton and we cheers to nothing because what else.

Alice Poem #4
I am going to have sex with someone else
for the first time in a long time and it is going
to be fucking wicked, okay? Underground
travel is the scariest bear when you are gone. How
we visited, threw one hundred pennies into
the Thames, drank rum, rode bronze lions. You
put cream on my hands when they came open and
were red. Maybe
if we crashed somewhere warm
it would be like
we didn't really crash. Send me an airbag
if you want. You can make it out of your stupid
massive cellulite thighs you fucking gay bitch.

29

In the taxi back, Macy falls asleep on my shoulder. Her hair folds into a cushion for my head. The driver asks if I had a good night, and I say yes. He says his football team fucked up today. I try to remember sports news. I don't say anything.

"Someone's a sleepy bunny," he says, turning to look at Macy when we get caught behind a coach on its way to Brussels.

I worry that he's going to rape us both, so I nudge Macy awake and push money into the cabbie's hand. We link arms and walk ten minutes back to the hotel. The lobby is empty except for its receptionist, reclining with a *Private Eye* propped in his lap. In the elevator Macy keeps her eyes closed and her arms around my middle. In the room, we make coffees to wake up a little. It's four. We sit cross-legged on the bed, with the television on and showing a long-haired man in a parka walking along the Jurassic coast, talking in hundreds of millions of years.

"I went there," I say. "It was a geography trip. Everyone got drunk and sneaked out of the hotel to swim. It was November, I think. I stayed in the room. I kept thinking about how currents would carry them out to sea and they'd all drown."

Nothing happens.

"Why are you so scared?" Macy asks.

"I don't know."

"You weren't scared tonight."

"Alex and Pablo were nice."

"Some people are. Not all strangers are scary. If you talk to people, they normally aren't."

I think about sitting in the bush with Amundsen while it rained and meeting Mabel. I think about talking about nothing but feeling like I'd been given emotional liposuction. "Sometimes people get abducted and murdered."

"If you don't try then you won't meet the ones that won't abduct or murder you. Would you have spoken to me if we'd met in a bar?"

"No."

"Are you happy we're here?"

"Yes."

She takes my mug and puts it next to hers on the

bedside table. Her mouth comes to mine. Our tongues wrestle. Macy's hands slide into the back of my hair. I fill my fist with her skirt. I feel like a child holding on to his mum in a thunderstorm. I move my hand up. I think, *These breasts have been restaurants.* I think, *Stop thinking that.* Macy pushes me down and climbs on top of me. Her skirt rides up past her knees and I glimpse the swarm of black pubes waiting behind her lace pants. I put my hands on her bum. I get a boner.

"I don't have a condom," I say.

"What?"

She's kissing my neck.

"I don't have a condom."

She stares at me and sits back. "I'm forty-six," she says. "We don't need a condom."

"I thought you were thirty-five."

"Why?"

"I don't know."

She gets off the bed and goes into the bathroom and locks the door. I sit up. I don't understand. She does look thirty-five, I feel. I'm not good at ages. She doesn't look forty-six. She definitely doesn't look forty-six. I thought women liked it when you said they look young. I thought it was the best compliment. Mum always drops coins when the man in Tesco asks her for ID as a joke.

Maybe she needed the toilet.

Maybe she's putting on sexy lingerie.

Something more comfortable.

I put my face against the bathroom door. "Are you okay?" I say.

"I'm okay," she says. It's difficult to make out what she's saying. "You should sleep. It's late." Her voice is wet. I don't know what I did. I did something wrong. Macy's upset, and it's because of me. This is why I shouldn't talk to people. Even nice people are bears when they make heavy weather happen in you.

I get into bed and pull the duvet over my head. I don't feel tired. I drink a Stella from the minibar and read about how to land hot-air balloons, make fire from rocks, and skin pigeons.

*

Macy fits herself in behind me. She shuffles her head and goes still. I'm the little spoon. Sometimes I pretend that the entire world is the big spoon, curling around me like a castle wall, endless and impenetrable.

"Thank you," she says.

I open my eyes. I can see drawings of crooked red flowers and cats on the wallpaper. The curtains are open and the black sky has peeled away, leaving behind a blue the color of flames on a gas hob. Macy's in her underwear. I can feel the damp warmth of her leg skin on mine. "Are you okay?" I say.

"Yes," she says. "I'm sorry for hiding. You made me panic."

"Sorry."

"No."

Nothing happens.

Macy rearranges herself. I can feel her breath tides going in and out of the hairs on my neck. She folds an arm over my chest. Her toes tickle the soles of my feet.

"Etgar," she says. "Can I say something?"

"Yes."

"You're young."

I try to laugh and shake my head. She can't see it and it isn't convincing. I stop trying to laugh. I say, "Okay, yes, I am." I awkwardly rotate my hand and lightly grab a fistful of her dress.

"How young?" She doesn't sound angry. She sounds curious and far away.

"Eighteen."

"Eighteen." Her finger traces my belly button. She forages in it. I think, *I hope I didn't leave anything in there.* "Eighteen is young."

"I know."

"I lied too."

"About what?"

"I don't have a business. I stay at home all day. I play Internet poker and watch porn. I don't know why I came here. It's partly you and partly home. Is this making sense to you?"

"Yes."

"I have a husband. I didn't tell him I was coming. I

just left." I roll over onto Macy. She grips my shoulder blades like stress balls. We are the only things left in the world. A zombie apocalypse has engulfed the planet, leaving only us intact. I feel like Macy has something else to say but she isn't going to say it. I don't mind.

"I feel calm," I say. "I don't feel anxious."

"Good."

The reason I'm calm is because of being honest, I think. I'm not having to hold and remember made-up things like being a mortgage broker and living in London. If you lie to people, then you expect people to lie to you back. Hattie. That is why I pretended to be Alice. I shouldn't have pretended to be Alice. If I hadn't pretended to be Alice then we would be lying in her bed watching the porn musical of *Alice in Wonderland* and drinking rum screwdrivers. Being dishonest makes me anxious, but I mostly want other people not to tell me the truth.

I lie on top of Macy and start to kiss her. My hands are flat on her temples. She cups my balls. I remember her saying about massive balls and I try not to laugh. I navigate her pants and slide a finger into her vag. It's extremely wet. It feels like uncooked bacon. I think, *Actual human children have fought their way out of this cave.* I think, *Stop thinking that.* Country house. Igloo. Puerto Rican driftwood.

30

Me and Alice were sitting under a web of blankets in her living room. It was the month we stopped leaving the house, except to visit her mum in hospital, and buy vodka, and spend whole days getting drunk in the cinema, moving from screen to screen without paying. I rolled over and said it was a bad blanket fort, that it was cramped and the ceilings were too low. Alice said it wasn't a blanket fort at all because we aren't American. She said it was a blanket castle.

"I'm bored," she said. Her head was in my lap. Keira Knightley was on the television, pushing out her jaw and kicking a football.

"Do you want to do sex?" I said. We had been doing sex an average of four times a day. It filled up the time, and Alice said it stopped her from thinking too much. School had sent folders of worksheets for us to do, but we made them into paper planes, then knocked them out of the air with deodorant flamethrowers.

"I don't know," she said. "Is there anything you want to try that we haven't?"

"Like what?" I pictured Alice choking me, hitting me, and whipping me. I pictured Mum visiting me in hospital, tutting, and saying "Kids these days" to a patronizing nurse who quickly leaves the room to dial social services. "No hitting."

"I didn't mean hitting."

"Then what?"

"I watched a golden shower thing the other day. The guy had like goggles on, and she did it on his face."

I laughed. "I don't know. Is that funny or disgusting?"

"Sexy."

"No. I don't know. There were like things I didn't like before you. So maybe."

She lifted her head off my lap.

"Like what?"

"Like tits. Also eating out."

"Don't call it that."

"What do I call it?"

"I don't know."

"Eating clams."

"No eating."

"Prawn cocktail."

"I'm breaking up with you," she said. "Unless we try it." I was drunk. I thought it might be fun, or not boring, or another, unidentified but positive feeling. I said yes. We had shots and went to the upstairs bathroom. I took off my clothes and lay in the bath. At least it would be washed away. I wondered briefly if you could die from urine. If it could sneak into my organs and rot them away.

"Do you remember when we were in Chris McDowell's bath?"

"You tried to fist me," she said. "Be still. I really need to go. There's going to be a lot."

"Can you die from urine?"

She pulled down her pants, threw them onto the toilet seat, and lifted one leg up and over me. "Where should I make it go?"

"This isn't . . . " She started pissing. It shot out of her in a straight, solid stream that looked like an umbilical cord connecting us. Alice as the mum. The piss was warm. It made me itchy. I didn't feel aroused.

She slipped. Her leg came off the lip of the bath and she fell to one side and piss went in my mouth. I shouted. I grabbed her thighs and pushed her back. "Mouth," I shouted.

"Okay," she said. She was grinning. She squatted and kept going. I wrestled her out of the bath, onto the floor, and pinned her hands to the tiles. I sat on her stomach and kissed her as hard as I could.

31

It's 10:15. My head is empty, then it's not. Check-out's at eleven. Macy's asleep. I tried to watch her sleeping because that's what romantic men do in films, but it was ultra-boring and I stopped. The sun's wide awake and the sky's doing a *today it will be warm* kind of blue. The window's slightly foggy. I turn on the TV. Macy makes a little sound. She doesn't wake up.

The bald man's inside the television. He's laughing with his co-presenter because she said *breast* instead of *best*. He looks at me and starts to talk. She takes a sip of coffee, starts to giggle, and sprays a fine brown mist.

"Okay," the bald man says. "A sports team played another sports team. Someone is still missing. Someone, somewhere, told a lie, about something boring and inconsequential. A person hit another person." I get up and take an orange juice out of the minibar. I sit on the edge of the bed and open it with my face close to the screen. The bald man touches his earlobe. "In other news," he says, "Etgar Allison has consummated his relationship with Macy Anderson, following a turbulent evening in which he befriended a homosexual couple and took three sips from a bottle of champagne before misguidedly attempting to emulate a Formula 1 victory." I smile. I don't remember doing that. The orange juice tastes sharp and foreign. "A miniature replica of Alice Calloway has been discovered inside his rib cage. Sources say the doll is shrinking and will continue to do so indefinitely. In a statement made earlier today, Allison likened himself to a zeppelin and claimed that he was 'feeling much better, thank you.' He has yet to confront Alice Calloway in person, and it remains unclear whether he will choose to do so."

I turn off the TV and stand in front of the window. A man in a vest top is unloading plastic crates from the back of a van. His body's short and his arms are long. Two people on rented bikes cycle past.

I play At Least. It's not heavy weather and I don't need to. Here:

– At least some humans want to sex me.

– At least other girls exist in the world.

– At least there will be a lot of tomorrows.

Macy yawns and flicks back a corner of the duvet. I

don't move from the window, because I want her to come up behind me and put her arms around my waist like in films. She puts her face into my hair. She puts her hand into my hand. The man in the vest wipes sweat from his forehead with the back of his arm. I turn and feel immediately like my body has been knotted.

Macy's upper arms and chest are dotted with purple bruises the size of ramekins. She looks at me looking at them. She doesn't say anything. I press my thumb against a dark spot on her ribs and gently trace the outline of it, wondering if it's possible to feel physical pain in that many places at once.

"Did you get mugged too?" I say.

"Kind of," she says.

"Did you get mugged by your husband?"

"Let's get breakfast. You'll be ill if you don't put something in your stomach."

"You don't want to talk about your husband."

"No, I don't." She winces and moves back to the bed, pulling on her hoodie and putting up the hood. She sits down. "I'm sorry," she says, putting her arms out in a *come and touch me* way. "I don't want to talk about him. He's not here."

"I know," I say. I climb onto her lap and put my head against her tits. "I'm sorry too. I want to be your husband. I want us to live in a tree house."

"I know," she says. "A tree house at the top of a redwood, without a ladder."

"And we have tiny planes to fly around in."

"Yes, we do."

"And I wear a fez."

"If you want."

"And you wear dungarees."

"Dungarees?" she laughs, blinks, and nods. "And I wear dungarees."

*

My train leaves at one. Macy's flight is at six. We're sitting on metal chairs outside a café called Ellen's. The air is so bright and clean it feels like we're somewhere in Europe. Paris or Berlin. Clouds race each other overhead. People with things to do and places to do them walk past. I look at their shoes. The shoes are always so shiny. I feel grateful that I don't have to spend any portion of my life polishing shoes. I have no idea why shoes are supposed to be shiny.

A waitress sets a tray down between us and unloads it. We both have lattes with toast. I take a bite and realize I'm not hungry and light a cigarette. Macy eats quietly, sometimes looking up to clean her lips with her wrist.

A cluster of pigeons gathers on the curb to stake out our crumbs. Most of them are cut or dented or missing feet. They slap each other with their wings.

"Don't you wish you had wings?" Macy says.

"No," I say. "That would be embarrassing. Everyone would stare. I wish I was taller."

"Don't say that. You're a fine size."

"You too." I take a sip of coffee and crush out my cigarette. "What are we going to do?" I say.

"I don't know."

"We could run to France. Or Cuba. Or Easter Island." I imagine us living under a tarpaulin in the shadow of a giant stone head. "Not Easter Island."

Macy peels the crust off a piece of toast and throws it toward the pigeons. They leap into a violent huddle, clubbing each other indiscriminately. "You know what would be best?" she says.

"What?"

"If I could go back in time and grow up with you."

I try to imagine it. A smaller, more smooth-skinned Macy drinking gin under the Christmas tree. We don't fit together. She tells me off like Alice, and it doesn't look right.

"Are you scared of going back?" I say.

"Yes."

'What will your husband do?'

"I don't know."

"Will he be angry?" She doesn't answer. I can see the shape of him in her eyes. A red, hunched man with wide shoulders and multiple rings. He beats his chest like a baboon. "Don't go back," I say.

"I have to."

"No, you don't. No one has to do anything. We're all going to die. Fuck everything."

Macy smiles. "You're still drunk," she says. She leans across the table and kisses me between the eyes.

"Am I ever going to see you again?" I say.

Macy does a *this laugh isn't a mean laugh* laugh. "Don't be melodramatic," she says. "This isn't a film. Yes. You will."

In the film version of right now, everything would turn black, one sentence would announce our unending happiness, and the credits would begin.

Macy takes out her phone, presses keys, and puts it away. "Let's stay another night," she says.

My heart goes double-time. "Really?"

"Yes, really."

"Where will we stay?"

"The hotel." I think about Gran's money. I think about how she died and how I'm going to die, painfully and unremarkably, and on a day a lot of days away from this one. We will both have infinity to be alone.

"So we have the whole today?"

"And the whole tonight."

"What should we do?"

"Whatever we want."

I decide I'm hungry now and eat my toast. Macy finishes hers. The pigeons quarrel and the sky fills with color and I try to think of places we can hide.

32

Me and Macy are facing each other, topless, and with bottles of Stella pressed against our chests. We are standing on our new hotel-room bed. Her sides are like the sides of a woman in a film who swims naked and makes the other characters feel insecure enough to begin diets. She nods at me. I shake my head.

"I can't," I say. "You go first."

She finishes the last of her beer and flicks the bottle onto the floor. She makes a Jesus shape with her body. Squares of muscle appear below her tits. "You have to go first."

"What if neither of us go first, we just climb under the duvet and watch David Attenborough?" I gently bounce. A trickle of Stella escapes my mouth and runs down my chin, throat, and chest.

"You asked what I wanted to do. This is what I want to do."

"I thought you'd want to go on the London Eye or binge-eat Mini Cheddars and watch TV."

"Are you saying I'm overweight?"

"What? No. You are not." She lunges forward and digs her fingers into my sides, tickling me until I topple onto the floor. I scream and thrash until she stops, her head resting against my collarbone and my head resting against the bedside table.

"So will you?" she says.

"Okay," I say.

We get back up and face each other again. I start to slowly count down from ten. At six, Macy tells me to stop. She points a finger at the blank skin over her belly button, closes her eyes, and says my name. I exhale.

I punch Macy in the stomach.

It is a harder punch than any of the punches I've done so far. I didn't mean it to be so hard. The sound that happens is like what I imagine a child would sound like hitting the pavement after falling three stories. Macy immediately crumples to the carpet. She curls up. I curl up next to her.

"I'm sorry," I say. "I'm sorry. I did it wrong."

She turns to face me and she's smiling, and she unfolds my hand, pressing it against where the punch connected.

I picture thousands of tiny people emigrating through my fingers, moving into her pores and pitching tents. I imagine them setting up a post office that we'll later use to communicate during heavy-weather nights.

Macy kisses me. "Your turn," she says. I stand up. I try to remember if you're supposed to tense the muscle or not tense it and I can't, but I decide to tense it anyway, because that looks best. It still doesn't look very good. There are only nine hairs connecting the waistband of my jeans and my belly button.

"Okay," I say. "Do it."

She does it.

Her fist drives all of the air out of my body and I fall forward and I wonder if I'm going to vomit. Purple stars and yellow planets drop into my eyes. I'm dizzy. I hold my stomach like a person in a war film trying to keep their bowels from escaping. "Help," I say. "Child abuse."

*

On the subway, Macy puts her hand underneath my T-shirt and rests it against the bruise. It feels familiar against the dull throbbing. No one is watching us. Everyone is watching their own feet. I push my cheek against Macy's cheek.

"This is really definitely what you want to do?" I say.

"Yes," she says. "I want one that makes sense."

"It's going to hurt."

"Less than the punching."

We get off after twenty minutes and walk without talking down a street of Victorian houses and patchwork pavement. It appears. Macy already phoned ahead, and the girl at the reception desk knows our names. She has an owl wearing glasses on her neck.

We fill out forms, and a man comes to tell us that his name is Mitch.

"What are we doing?" he says. There is an upturned umbrella under his left eye, a swallow on his hand, and a tiger on his Adam's apple. I take a step back.

I lift up my T-shirt, nod, and drop it. "The outline of that bruise," I say. "Please."

Nothing happens.

"The bruise," he says. "In black?"

"Yes."

"Okay."

We move to a giant chair. Mitch gestures at me to take off my T-shirt and I do, feeling conspicuously tiny and underweight. He doesn't notice. He roughly shaves the nonexistent hair over the bruise on my belly with a disposable plastic razor.

"What made you want this?" he says.

"Um," I say.

"I *ummed* once. Look." He pulls up his trouser leg and prods a squirting purple dick with eyes and lipstick. It is crisscrossed with bursting veins, cuts, and hairs.

I swallow. "Very cool," I say. "Very cool tattoo."

"Not really."

"No, I mean. Yes. Not cool at all. Medium cool. Not cool and not, not cool."

"Right." He blinks at me and shakes his head. He thinks I have special needs. I do have special needs. Macy is one of them. "You ready?"

"Ready as I'll ever be."

"Yes or no?"

"Yes."

He wipes jelly over the ink and starts to follow the outline. It doesn't hurt like I thought it would. It feels like a small trail of burning. I watch the line form and feel warm knowing it won't ever leave. My skin will stretch and shed, and my bones will grow, but the edge of this bruise will stay the same. Macy stands behind me, her hand resting in my hair.

"You're done," he says, after not many minutes. "Now it's Mum's turn."

"She's not my mum."

Macy shakes her head and laughs. "Kids," she says. "They hit a certain age and it's like they don't want to know you anymore." She grins. Mitch smiles and shakes his head at me like I'm his son. I'm not his son. I'm Dad's son.

When hers is finished, we stand in front of the mirror.

"Yours looks like Alaska," Macy says.

"Yours looks like a panda," I say, imagining each word is the name of an invincible superhero.

33

We buy beer, paper, scissors, glue, and several home and lifestyle magazines from a Tesco near the hotel. When we get inside, we immediately undress and climb back into bed, peeling the sheets of cellophane away from our tattoos. We use bedside tables to prop the duvet up from inside. We sit in the tent and touch each other's faces. I hold her jaw lightly in cupped hands, like a hamster. Macy grips my wrists and tells me to wait.

"Okay," she says. "The first rule is that nothing outside of this tent exists."

"Not even Ariana Grande."

"Especially not Ariana Grande."

"Bye, Ariana."

"The second rule is that you can only make it out of

things from the magazines." She tucks a band of hair behind her ear. Under the thick light her face looks like a sepia photograph. "But you can arrange them any way you want."

"Can there be celebrities?"

"Yes. But no kissing them."

"I don't even want to."

She leans in and kisses me. "Okay. So we have the pictures and we connect them up anyway we want. It has to be about you too, though, not just us. You need a job, remember."

"To support you."

"Yes."

"Okay."

"Ready?"

"Yes."

*

I will wake up refreshed and alert in a room that smells of lake water and butter. You will be asleep on your back. I will kiss your eyebrows, move into the kitchen, and sip coffee prepared by our friendly robot maid, Dolores. The view from the window over our empty sink will be of a morning the color of peppermint, happening over flat, endless ocean.

I will think about boats, your feet, and redecorating the bathroom.

I will idly push my finger against dates on the calendar. *Sarah wedding. Tom birthday. Katie baptism. Leave for NY. Back from NY. Dentist. TV interview. Knighting ceremony.*

I will leave for work.

My job will be to sit in a cushion pit, watching unreleased films and suggesting improvements.

More touching. Less cancer. A joke about manatees.

My colleagues will be quiet and unserious. On work trips with shared hotel rooms, we will pile up our mattresses and jump from increasingly dangerous heights. We will empty our minibars and become wildly honest.

Me and Robert Pattinson will play tennis together every other weekend. He will have an extremely strong serve. Over post-match drinks, we will plan a weeklong camping trip to the Italian Alps. We will talk about snow and sap and how quickly our calves will turn to tightly strung bows.

My chauffeur will drive me home along neon-heavy streets under light rain. His name will be Sebastian. He will enjoy sushi, latex, and the films of Sion Sono. We will stop briefly for tangerines, then leave the city. I will text you a photo of the back of Sebastian's head with my face reflected in it.

Our house will be a large but not blatant network of tree houses in a forest forty miles from the nearest building. It will consist of various large wooden structures linked by rope bridges.

*

"Wait," I say. "What about your kids?"

"Nothing else exists, remember."

"I keep imagining them starving to death somewhere that doesn't have you in it."

"They've been abducted and killed."

"That's too much."

"Abducted and never heard of again."

"Okay."

*

You will meet me midway along the entrance bridge. While hugging you, I will frantically rock the bridge and you will scream and tell me to stop, but you will be joking and I will continue.

We will sit at opposite ends of baths late at night, drinking rum and purposely getting film quotes wrong. We will shampoo each other's hair. You will gently press out the blackheads on my back and you will tell me that it's normal and you will not be revolted.

We will ingest Nytol and sleep for fifteen-hour stretches. During periods of heavy rain, we will become immobile and childish. We will communicate with animal sounds and hand-squeezing.

On warm days, you will be silent while I apply sun cream to your cheeks. We will smoke cigarettes and whip each other with tree branches, hard enough to be fun but not hard enough for bruises. We will eat jam sandwiches and pre-made fruit salads.

You will take up knitting, knit something you insist is a tabard, and give away all the remaining wool.

We will quit our jobs and retire in a politically stable country where people take afternoon naps and eat outside. We will learn bridge, yoga, and scuba diving.

We will die simultaneously.

*

"I don't like Dolores," Macy says. "No more Dolores. She's creepy."

"Okay."

She laughs and falls forward over our collection of damp collages. I plant my hands on her arms and we roll over, and the bedside tables fall to the carpet.

34

When it's over, we open the curtains and build high pillow mounds to recline on. Lines of people in revealing clothes fill up the street, and tall buildings start to glow. I think about how many people are in the buildings, then I stop because it's too many. I turn on the TV.

"What do you want to watch?" I say.

"I don't know."

Love Actually is on, but it's already been on for a while and Colin Firth is already sprinting to Portugal to propose. I don't change the channel. I can't concentrate.

"Do you think we should be honest?" I say.

"No." She bites her nail. "What do you mean?"

"About stuff."

She exhales and slumps forward. "No," she says.

"That would ruin it. There's no reason why you need to know that I work in a school or own a Hyundai, because it doesn't affect me, and you, and now, which is honestly . . . no, it sounds stupid."

"It doesn't sound stupid."

I don't know why she's telling me she has a Hyundai if she doesn't want me to know she has a Hyundai.

"You don't know what it is."

"You never sound stupid."

Except when you talk about big balls.

"I feel happy today."

"Me too."

Nothing happens.

"Um. You work in a school," I say. "I thought you stayed at home."

"Holidays. I don't feel like it matters, everyone's lying to everyone else all the time anyway. It's better for us to make up lies together."

I think about Hattie. Honesty as a piñata. A huge, garish, donkey-shaped piñata that everyone is smacking with bare hands, hoping it splits open and leaks tiny lumps of something better than whatever they already have.

"I think so too."

"You want to say something?"

I tip my head back and look at hers. It seems too still and calm to be alive, like it's the head of a serene Indian god cast in copper. I swallow. "I'm fifteen," I say.

She sighs. "I'm not stupid."

"No, really, I am."

"I meant I know you are."

"Oh."

"I'll turn myself in and go to prison. They'll give me eight years. It will be front-page news. They'll say I lured you to a hotel room." She rearranges herself so that her face is on my belly button, her eyes pointed up and toward me.

"You didn't even groom me," I say. "I paid for everything."

"They'll say I manipulated you."

"Did you?"

"Maybe."

I mute the TV. "In prison, the not-pedophile inmates throw acid in the pedophile inmates' faces."

"I'll pretend to be a murderer."

"I don't want them to do that to you."

"I know." She maneuvers herself onto me and slides down my boxer shorts, and I can see the shapes of ceiling lights reflected in her hair.

In the morning, Macy's gone and there's a note: *I didn't really want to say good-bye. I'm sorry. Let's talk tonight.*

On the train home, I write a letter and fall asleep. I dream about dead dogs, a safari, and hurricanes.

Macy Poem #1
In the event of a zombie apocalypse
in which you were a zombie
my plan would be
to eat three bars of Galaxy
drink six cups of tea
and lie somewhere
clearly visible
but vaguely comfortable
and not try to decapitate you
or stop you from infecting me
with zombie virus.

PART 4

Birthmark

35

The house is filled with wind. I left the conservatory
doors open for Amundsen, who's been sleeping on my
bed and shedding on my carpet. I say sorry. He pants
and salivates and licks my eyebrows. I tell him we can
go for a walk after I've tidied. There's a lot to tidy. There
are empty bottles and unwashed plates and chunks of
smashed glass on the linoleum. I don't remember
smashing glass. I check Amundsen's paws for splinters.
He's okay. Alive. I fill two bin bags with rubbish and
stack up the washing, thinking I'll do it later and knowing
I won't.

The kettle boils.

I make a Nesquik tea and drink it on the sofa, under
a blanket thick with dog hair. There's a film on about a

man and a woman who fall in love and then the woman disappears and the man tries to find her. He doesn't know if she's been murdered or kidnapped. He tells everyone that she wouldn't have run away. He sells his house and his car and hires detectives. In the end, she appears and says she loves him and they get married. She doesn't say where she's been. I think, *This is stupid.* Maybe I missed something. It makes me sleepy, though, because they're smiling a lot at the end. I feel like the last four days have lasted forty days. They're getting married in a park now. I don't know if that's legal. I'm almost asleep then Amundsen starts pestering me to take him for a walk. I yawn. I check the time on my phone.

"If you wait ten minutes, we'll see Mushroom." He climbs onto the sofa and rests his head on my crotch.

*

There's a little Famous Grouse left and I drink it. I need to be brave. I need to go and do a sorry to Aslam. I fill my backpack with a flash drive loaded with Greta Gerwig mumblecores, Dad's sloe vodka, strawberry Nesquik, and four Typhoo teabags (Aslam's family uses loose tea. It tastes bad with Nesquik). Amundsen's tired. He's asleep in the armchair. I empty a can of tripe into his bowl and leave.

Aslam lives in a house with his dad and little brother, Thayyab, next to the cemetery at the bottom of the hill.

There's no car outside, so his dad must be at work. I push the recycling bin up to the side gate and climb over. I shuffle along the concrete and look through the kitchen window. There's an overflowing ashtray, a half-drunk bottle of rosé, chocolate fingers, and no Aslam. I wonder who's been drinking gay wine. I prop the window open on its metal stem and slide myself in through the gap. I land with my feet in the sink.

He must be in his room building computers. He probably has headphones on. I can come up from behind and give him a heart attack. He'll be excited about getting to go to the hospital, and he'll forgive me. Aslam was in St. James for a week last year with a broken collarbone. He told me it was fucking wicked. Free food and fit nurses, he said.

I down some of the rosé and eat a chocolate finger, then go upstairs. Aslam's door is the one past the bedroom. Thayyab writes notes and sticks them to his brother's door depending on how he feels toward him. Today the sign is written in green highlighter.

big gay prikheds room

I gently push open the door and stop. The curtains are drawn and a paper floor lamp that looks like a dystopian cocoon is glowing by the bed.

I immediately feel physically ill.

My chest crushes itself.

I can hear the blood beating in my head.

Alice's back is to me. It is frantically bobbing up and

down. She's naked except for a plastic clip holding her hair together on top of her head. It's probably so she could suck him off. She's doing sex moans that sound like snoring lions. Aslam's fingertips appear on either side of her waist. They squeeze until blood drives away from them and the skin turns white.

My lethargy evaporates. I feel like I'm everywhere. I take a potted plant down from a bookshelf and advance on them. He sees me before I get close enough. He screams and spins. The girl jumps up, pulling the duvet over her breasts.

The girl isn't Alice.

I don't recognize the girl.

She's fit.

An eight maybe.

"Etgar," Alslam says.

"Uh."

"What the fuck is wrong with you?"

"I'm going to throw up."

He throws a trash can at me, and I catch it. The last four days fall out of my mouth. The last four days are sour neon soup. My stomach spasms and cries. I open my eyes. The trash can is a wire trash can. Lumps of sick spot the carpet.

"Were you going to kill me?" Aslam says.

"No."

"Because it kind of looks like you were going to kill me, man."

I put the trash can down. "I thought she was Alice."

"She looks nothing like Alice."

He's right. Her nose is longer and she barely has eyebrows. "I know. She's not Alice. I'm kind of drunk."

"This is Amy. I told you about Amy." I should have listened. I should have clicked the links to videos he sent. I should have helped him meet and seduce her at the Monopoly party.

"Oh."

"Etgar, Amy. Amy, Etgar."

We shake hands. She does a little laugh and smiles an *I don't know what's happening* smile. Her hand is wet with sex sweat.

"I was coming over to say sorry. I'm sorry. I brought Nesquik and Greta Gerwig."

"Jesus. It's okay. Let me punch you and we'll be even. Just stop being mental. I probably shouldn't have kept trying to make you come out. It's just boring now, no one will go out with me."

Amy shifts uncomfortably.

"Oh," I say. "Sorry. I'll let you finish."

"I've gone soft," Aslam says. Amy laughs. "Let's get dressed. Did you bring anything that isn't Nesquik to drink?"

"I brought sloe vodka."

"What the fuck is that?"

"It's like . . . uh. You put berries in vodka and then leave it for ages."

"Sweet," Aslam says. "Wash your face and put the TV on."

"Okay. Thanks. Sorry."

I go downstairs. I feel light and excited to sit somewhere warm, get drunk, and watch films. There is nothing bad left to happen. I'm already drunk. I haven't stopped being drunk since whatever day it was I started getting drunk. The news comes on. More bad things are happening in faraway places. The bald man isn't there. He's retired. He's gone to open a rum bar with his wife in the Mediterranean.

I go through Aslam's DVD tower. I choose *Aristocats*. It's got songs in it and no one dies at the end. Alice and I never watched it together. Aslam is the only person who ever really wanted to see Disneys.

When he comes down, Aslam gets shot glasses and we arrange ourselves on the sofa cushions, under an unzipped sleeping bag. Constavlos curls up in the armchair. We talk while the film plays. Amy sings to some of the songs, and I decide that I like her. She says that she made a video of herself singing "Ev'rybody Wants to Be a Cat" and it got fifty thousand views on YouTube. She says that when she broke up with her last boyfriend he crashed his car into her garage and got his hand stuck in her mailbox. Police and firemen had to come. They cut him out.

We laugh.

The laughter dissolves.

"What did she do?" Amy says.

I fidget. "She handjobbed someone with a tribal tattoo then told me he raped her with kisses."

Amy and Aslam lock eyes. She bats her eyelashes.

"We could egg her," she says.

"Yes," I say. "No. I don't know."

"Say yes. We won't get caught. If we do, you can tell her dad what she did." I think, *I like Mr. Calloway. He didn't give Aaron Mathews a handjob. He shouldn't have his house egged.* Once, while Alice was asleep, I went downstairs to get a beer. Mr Calloway was sitting at the marble island in their kitchen, eating Weetabix and reading a book. He stood up. His dressing gown was heavy with the weight of the chocolate Hobnobs in its pockets. "Are you okay?" I said. "It's hard to be away from each other," he said. We hugged, and my forehead got wet from the sweat on his chest.

I think, *It would definitely make me feel better to egg her house.*

"Yes," I say. "Okay."

We wait for nighttime, then go to the corner store and buy twelve eggs, three tall bottles of Kronenbourg, and wine gums. Alice's house is ten minutes away, in the new subdivision by the primary school. Her dad's car isn't in the driveway. Aslam hands out eggs and does a count-down. On three, we throw and I laugh because it's stupid and I feel good and I don't know why, but Aslam's not having sex with Alice and everything might be fine.

The house looks like it has acne.

Okay, not fine. But better.

I tell Aslam and Amy to go home and finish having sex. I say thanks. Amy tells me to forget Alice. I tell her to forget that I tried to kill them.

36

Me and Alice were drinking Strongbow on a concrete ledge by the beach in Brighton. June. The sun was alone and close. Specks of salt and sea fell down over our heads and our bangs were being pulled to one side and we were smoking. It was a Monday. It was a school day, but Alice's brother had called in. He said that their mum's cooking had given us both food poisoning. Age fourteen. Her mum wasn't dying. We'd taken the day off because Alice had her second abortion the day before. We'd called it Malcolm after *Malcolm in the Middle*. We'd called the first one Albus.

Alice leaned back against my chest. Her hair smelled like just-blown-out candles. She had panda eyes. She looked sexy when she was emotionally distressed, but I was still wishing that she wasn't.

I watched a dog chase a bird. I watched a man chase a dog. I watched the sea carry on and carry on, and a boat passed along the edge of it and the waves made *sh* sounds. My head got warm from the cider. I went quiet inside. A tiny me shuffled onstage, scratching his hands and blinking too much. Doing a *this isn't a real smile* smile. I knew it was stupid, but I felt too heavy not to write little letters.

Hi Little Mate,

It's heavy weather here today. Sorry you didn't get to visit. Honestly, it's not that good anyway. I know you should have been able to decide, though. Some people like it, I guess. Rebecca Talbot smiles almost constantly. She wears primary colors and never hides. I've seen her cry at happy things. Dolphins and people who win against cancer.

I don't know.

It's hard to tell.

Sometimes things are okay. Sometimes you get to stay in bed all day. Sometimes coffee actually tastes good. Sometimes you can sit down in the shower and pretend to be in a monsoon. Sometimes sex lasts longer than a TV advert. Sometimes, after dinner, the sky goes funny colors and it looks like an aquarium filled with Nemos. Sometimes the people next to you don't make you want to eat your own hands. Sometimes sleep is easy. Sometimes there's Alice. Sometimes you don't have enough money, but the man in the shop lets you have the cigarettes anyway. Sometimes it's warm and you're drunk and you're tall.

Mostly though, it's scary. People hit you and rob you and die next to you.

I wonder if you'd have been scared like me, or loud like Alice. I wonder if you'd have grown up to be something proper like a fireman or a carpenter. Do carpenters even exist now? Probably not. I want to think that you'd grow up to do something that would benefit humanity. I also want to think that you'd grow up to be nothing. To be one of those people who dies alone in a council house and is found three years later, partially eaten and surrounded by dead cats. If I think about that then it makes me feel less bad about you not arriving. I don't know.

Sorry. You wouldn't have been that.

You would have been a teacher, at least.

Or a dentist.

This is starting to sound gay. I don't normally sound like Jodi Picoult. Sorry again. And if you see Albus, say hi. He'll help if you're lost.

Be okay.

Night-night.

People started to get out of school. They were walking in sets behind us, typing into phones and laughing. They felt far away, like uninterested aliens we were watching from our own personal planet. I found Alice's belly button under her hoodie and pushed my finger into it. She squirmed but didn't stop me. She was in a quiet mood and hadn't yet told me off for anything.

"You should get an implant," I said.

"I will," she said.

"Like soon."

"I know. I will."

A woman with a toddler stopped near us. She unwrapped an ice cream sandwich and passed it down to him. He looked at Alice and smiled. She did a tiny wave.

"He wouldn't be smiling if he knew what you did to people like him." She simultaneously punched my thigh and kissed my ear. I imagined Malcolm as a miniature adult that we'd put into a spaceship and sent away. I imagined his tiny, unformed limbs tumbling through infinite blackness.

We napped on the train home and spent the evening in bed watching mondo films. *Faces of Death*, *Traces of Death*, *Faces of Gore*, *Mondo Cane*. *Mondo Cane 2*. *Mondo Cane 3*. *Mondo Cane 4*. Compilations of clips of people dying in gory ways. I think the best way to escape in your head isn't to think about things that aren't real, it's to think about things that are and then imagine them happening to people who aren't you.

37

I'm cleaning Alice's house with an old mop I found under the stairs. I couldn't sleep. I was anxious. I kept imagining Mr. Calloway stepping out of his car and sighing and heavy weather happening in his head. I kept thinking about Alice's mum and Albus and Malcolm. They're at home, so I'm being quiet. The eggs are almost gone.

The front door opens. I think about running and know that I won't try.

It's Alice.

"Etgar?" she says.

"Oh, hi." I lay the mop down and put my hands in my pockets. There are three coins in the left one and a wad of crumpled receipts in the other.

She stays in the doorway. "What are you doing?"

"Cleaning your house."

"Why?"

"It has egg on it."

"Oh."

"I'm sorry. It was Aslam's idea. He has a girlfriend. She has like fifty thousand views on YouTube."

"Oh."

"I wrote you a letter."

"Are you drunk?"

"A little." She comes close. We are lit up by one streetlight and the blue glow of the TV from her bedroom window. I can see the black pits in her nose like strawberry skin. She's not wearing any makeup. I think, *I'm going to miss you.* I push the paper into her hand.

"Etgar, I'm really sorry."

"I know. I did a letter."

"It's going to be weird."

"I know."

"Do you want to be friends?"

"I cover that in the letter."

"Why are you talking like that?"

"I don't know how to talk."

"The same as you talked before."

"Okay." Nothing happens. "See you at school."

Her eyes are wobbling. I want to step forward and grab her head and put it against my head. I know I won't do that. I know we'll grow taller and farther away and we'll be adults and this will be a tiny corner of our lives that gets forgotten except for certain days under certain lights when it rises like a hot-air balloon from endless forest.

"Okay," she says. She blinks. A tear comes out of one eye. She turns around. She goes back into the house. I realize that talking like we don't know each other has been the heaviest weather. I want to go home. I want to sleep everything away. I kick four stones at some railings. A car goes past. Alice's TV turns off.

*

Aslam lets me sleep at his house. Amy's still there. He doesn't ask what's wrong. Me and his little brother sit watching *CSI: Miami* in the living room. Thayyab wears monkey pajamas and I wear Thayyab's Power Rangers duvet.

"I think that one did it," he says, pointing out a skinny man with cuts around his eyes. "He's the one."

"Yeah," I say. "He's the one."

*

Dear Alice,

It's me, Etgar, writing from beyond the grave. Because I killed myself. Because you gave Aaron Mathews a handjob.

Joking.

Hi.

I'm sorry for calling you a walrus. You are not a walrus. If anything, you're underweight. Not in a close-to-death way. It's attractive. Like a model. You know that. I was being drunk and upset. It didn't mean anything. Your body is a good shape and size. I'm being honest.

I'm also sorry for going on to your Facebook and pretending to be you so that Marie would tell me what had happened. I wish I hadn't done that. It's too late. Please don't blame Marie. We were together for three years, and I can do an excellent impression of you. Here:

I miss you come over!!!!! we can drink Fanta and watch *Buffy*. I got a new duvet so we have 2xxxxxxxx.

Sorry, that was mean. I'm still a little drunk.

I am very scared about not being your boyfriend anymore. You were like a sexy foster mum to me. The world seems big and angry again. I am scared but I also think that maybe it's a good thing. If you kissed Aaron Mathews, it was because you wanted to. You were drunk, but you wanted to. I understand. He has very large feet and symmetrical features. It's okay, I want to kiss other people sometimes too. And that probably means we only stayed together because it felt comfortable and familiar and safe. I said *only*. That seems like the wrong word. I think *partly* might be a better word (actually, *ratatouille* is a much better word than both of them, but it doesn't really fit).

You know that we were never going to get married and have a baby and buy a house and be buried next to each other. It's hard to think that far ahead but sometimes useful to try.

(For reference, if I die without a will, please mix my ashes with tripe and feed them to Amundsen. My tiny people are already friendly with his tiny people, and I know that he'd be more than willing to take them on. I'll be in his blood and drool. If you need me for anything, you can ask him.)

(Oh, so you know, I'm not planning on dying soon. I read about suicide on the Internet and it seemed ultra-scary.)

(Sorry for all these parentheses. It's hard writing on paper. You can't delete things and I don't have any Wite-Out.)

We were together for 1,037 days. I just counted. That's a lot of days. In those days your tits happened and my dick went kind of brown and we both got taller and sat exams. I think that means it's different to other times when we'll go out with people. Going out with other people seems impossible to imagine. I don't know. Everyone is scared of disappearing things, I feel.

That's why in films people say "Let's be friends" when they break up. I don't think we should be friends, because I've seen your vagina and it would be awkward. When I forget how it looks, we can be friends. We might be old. We might have espresso machines. I don't want an espresso machine, Alice. I really don't.

This all seems big, and it happened really fast. This letter was stupid. I'm sorry. It's hard to know what things to say or whether to say anything.

Be okay,

Etgar

38

Mum and Dad are sitting on the sofa watching *The Voice* on Netflix. Mum stands up when I come in.

"I broke up with Alice," I say. I say it immediately, because if you say something at the wrong time then you don't have to spend time looking for the right time to say it. "No biggie." It feels like someone else has said the words "No biggie." I don't understand why I would say "no biggie." Who am I? I turn around, but there's no one else there.

"Oh, darling," Mum says. She hugs me hard. "I'm sorry." Dad stands up and claps my shoulder and walks through to the toilet. He doesn't like to watch when me and Mum talk about emotions with each other. "Are you okay?" Mum says.

"Yes."

Mum tries to say other tender things, but when Dad uses the toilet he makes the sound that female tennis players make. She puts me on the sofa and asks if I want anything. I try to ask about Russia. She says we can talk about that later.

"Do you want me to drive to Blockbuster and get something with that girl you like in it?" she says.

"Yes, please. Not *(500) Days of Summer*."

*

I spend the day on the sofa drinking water. Drinking for four days without stopping has made me tired and psychotic. I watch four episodes of *Community* and read some of *Cat's Cradle* and watch a video of a man suiciding on webcam. Macy isn't online. I imagine her standing over a pan of risotto. I imagine her groping her husband's giant balls and wiping dirt from the faces of her children. I hope she's alive and okay.

I nap.

Amundsen wakes me up with his tongue.

We nap.

Mum wakes me up with Zooey Deschanel. She's rented *Our Idiot Brother*, which has Paul Rudd and Rashida Jones in it too, so I'm excited. We watch it together, spread out under blankets across the sofas. Dad says things about tearing new assholes in all the women. Mum laughs and hits him. Incidentally, the film is extremely disappointing.

*

Dad comes into my room. It's ten. I'm talking to Connie Latterly about the Nibiru cataclysm and editing the Wikipedia pages of famous footballers to say that they are all distantly related to Barack Obama.

"Dad, don't be a pedo. Get out." I shut the laptop and put it on the carpet. I'm tired.

"I wasn't going to touch." He takes off his glasses, breathes on the glass, and rubs them with the corner of his shirt.

"Stay over there, or I'm calling Pedoline."

"Pedoline isn't a thing."

"Firemen then."

"Why would you call firemen?"

"Firemen hate pedos. They shoot them with their hoses."

Dad laughs and sits down on the end of my bed. It sinks under his weight, and my legs fall into the valley he's made. "Are you okay?"

"I don't know. I drank your Famous Grouse. It was disgusting. Why is the grouse famous?"

"Because it discovered America. I'm sorry about Alice. Try not to let it ruin everything. There are still plenty of girls out there, and most of them have bigger bosoms."

"Bosoms?"

"You know what I mean. Boobs."

"I don't like big tits anyway."

"Pedo."

"Dad."

He takes his glasses back off his head, folds them up, and sets them down on his lap. "I remember losing my first girlfriend. I remember feeling like everything was over."

"What happened?"

"She hung herself. It was very odd. She was always saying things like 'I want to die,' and everyone thought she was joking. She was a pretty funny girl actually."

"How old were you?"

"Twelve."

"Dad, that's not funny."

"It's not a joke."

"Oh."

Dad smiles. "You just need to remember to check you've got your limbs and your torso and your face. You're alive. You'll keep being alive for quite a while longer. Everything that will happen to you has already happened to me and to your mum and to your granddad. And we all survived. For now. There are no new problems, only new ways of solving them." I don't think that means anything, or is related, but it sounds good.

"Puberty."

"I was thinking about girlfriends and drink and acne."

"I have miraculously clear skin."

"I know. I used to put toothpaste on mine."

"I feel bad for feeling bad about it. Like, that there are children starving in Africa and stuff."

"The fact that humans haven't yet managed a global redistribution of wealth is never going to lessen the hurt in your little heart."

"I don't have hurt in my little heart."

"I know."

"Really, I'm feeling better."

"I'm glad."

"I met someone else."

"Lovely."

He leans forward to pinch my cheek. I shout "pedo." Mum pushes open my door and curls her neck around it.

"What are you two up to?"

"Dad said 'This is what adults do when they love each other' to me, and then he touched me."

"Etgar, don't be disgusting."

"Arrest him, Mum."

"*Casualty's* starting, darling."

"Okay. I'll be down in a sec." They nod at each other like people about to carry out a secret plan.

"Night-night," Mum says. "I love you."

"You too."

She leaves.

"You'll be okay," Dad says. "Won't you? No hanging or anything?"

"Yes. But . . . I did something bad." I chew the duvet. Some poppers come undone. They taste like stale sweat.

"Okay."

"I spent a lot of the Nan money. I think I spent a thousand pounds."

Dad bites his lip and tilts his head. "Don't worry. At least you're alive. You try and find a part-time job and save up a little each week."

"Don't you want to know what I spent it on?"

"I don't know. Do I?"

"Maybe not."

"Okay. Don't do it again. Unless it was an uncharacteristically generous donation to charity."

"I won't. It wasn't."

"Good. See you in the morning."

"Night."

"Night."

He leaves quietly, closing the door behind him. His socks are violently odd. I push Amundsen over to the radiator side of the bed, pull the duvet up, and think to myself, *See you in the morning.*

PART 5

Antlers

39

"Is this true?" Mum says. "Is what these people are saying true?" She's standing in my bedroom, between two police officers, holding her own hands. Her eyes are stretched wide and close to leaking. I'm trying not to look. I'm imagining myself in a warm, dark chamber, hidden beneath the deepest ocean's bed, building matchstick models of poodles and eating fistfuls of prosciutto. "Etgar?"

"No," I say, pulling the duvet over my mouth. "It wasn't that. They're making it up. This doesn't make sense. She didn't do anything."

"She touched you."

"Mum, please stop." This is the most embarrassing thing to have happened during the whole time that I've existed. I don't know how it happened. They won't let me think. I think, *Maybe it was the Internet police, or guilt, or Macy's husband.* I don't think it was guilt. I'm not entirely sure the Internet police exist.

"She did."

I force my head up and point my eyes at the tallest police officer. "What are you talking about? I touched her too. Why can't people touch each other?"

"You poor thing," Mum says. She sits down on the bed next to me and tries to pull me in to her. I push her away. Dad's standing behind the policemen, with his hands behind his back, looking at a stain on the ceiling. I want him to understand. I want him to explain that this is a misunderstanding and ask them all to please leave. I don't know what's happening in his head, but I don't want him to think I'm smaller than he already does. Nothing appears in his eyes. He leaves the room and walks downstairs.

"Stop," I say. "This is fucked."

"Language, Etgar."

"But it is. It's so fucked that you think Uncle Michael marrying a woman he bought off the Internet is fine, but if I meet a woman who stops me from feeling alone, then the police come around because she's old." The police officers look at each other, and one sighs, and the other bites his lip. "She's not even really old."

"Your Uncle Michael did not buy Alena. And that woman took advantage of you. You probably don't understand yet."

"Yes he did, and yes I do." I'm shouting. I stand up. I should throw something, for effect. In the film version of right now, this would be the part with the murder. This would be the part where I break down and punch inanimate objects until I fall unconscious, blood running out of my knuckles. "He's paying for a woman to live with him because he's old and pathetic and lonely. I'm trying not to be. This is stupid."

"Don't talk about your uncle like that."

"Don't talk about Macy like that."

"Like what?"

"Like she did something wrong." I run out of the room, knocking the police officers' shoulders and tripping slightly on the stairs. Dad's on the sofa, watching a blank TV. He doesn't move when I pass him. I hope he heard. I hope he doesn't think that I'm the type of child to be unwittingly groomed and used by a pedophile. I hope he realizes that I have decided to start shouting.

It's warmer outside. I go to the field. A couple with two golden retrievers are hurling Frisbees through the sky and four boys are smoking by the oak tree. I locate the gap in the hedges where Amundsen and I hid from rain, and I fit myself in and sit down on the bank of mud. It's unstable from days of rain. I pull my T-shirt up over my face and gently trace laps of Alaska.

I picture a sequence of time-lapse photos on a night-time motorway, with me unmoving between the streams of headlights. I picture a car swerving dumbly into me and my bleeding body being knocked into a ditch. I picture Macy being led away from her house. I picture the tree house and I imagine its windows made dark with metal bars.

"Oh dear," a voice says. "Someone looks underneath the weather." I feel the weight of a small dog settle in my lap. "Are you okay? Should I give you advice? I suppose that's what old people are for. Good evening."

"Um. Hi." I wipe a length of snot from my nose and take my head out of my T-shirt.

Mabel's pulling a leaf apart in her hands. "So," she says. "What sort of advice would you like?"

"I'm not sure."

"To hell with it!"

"What?"

"To hell with it!"

"Um."

"It's not too good, is it? I expected I might say something more insightful, to be totally honest with you, Etgar." Mushroom rears up and drops his paws on my knees. He licks the gap between my thumb and index finger.

"It's okay."

"And nap."

"What?"

"Take naps."

"Okay."

"Is that useful?"

"Not really. Also yes, in general, but not now."

"The pen is mightier than swords."

"Sorry."

"Let sleeping dogs do what sleeping dogs want to do."

"I'm not sure that's one."

"I'm sorry. I'm beginning to think there isn't any particularly useful advice anywhere in me."

"What would you do if you really liked someone but the police put the someone in jail?"

She drops the leaf and bites her lower lip. Her eyelids droop slightly. Mushroom does a whine. "Be very angry," she says. I nod. I don't know how to be angry, but I think it will happen, grandly, and in one step, like reaching the moon. I say good-bye. I go home and try not to look at Mum. I leave with the police officers.

40

We're sitting in a row on the sofa, watching a program about assisted suicide and passing a bowl of stale corn-flakes between us. There was nothing else in the kitchen, and no one wanted to go outside. It's eight and the sky is starting to roll down. Mum tried to talk with me about Macy, but her mouth didn't make the right words, and she sounded like a deaf person, so we turned on the TV and watched the first thing that appeared.

A silver-haired talking head says that death is a right, and it should be available to everyone, instead of only people rich enough to fly to Switzerland. There are shots of the room where it happens. It's small and painted impersonal colors.

Dad nods. "Would you kill me if I asked?" he says.

"I'd shoot you in the face," I say. "If you asked."

"Where would you get a firearm?"

"I'd just do it with a catapult and a rock."

"Stop it," Mum says. She stands up and goes to the window, pressing her face and hands against the glass.

"And if I wasn't of sound mind?"

"I wouldn't be able to tell probably. I'd do it anyway."

Mum turns and tells Dad off again, saying that he shouldn't be saying things like that. Turning back, she freezes. A bright, sudden flash fills the room, blanking everything out for a quarter of a second. Mum snaps the curtains closed. "Oh my Jesus wept," she says. "Pete, there's a man outside our house."

"What man?"

"I don't know what man. How do I know what man? He took a photo."

"A journalist," I say.

She plants her hands on her hips. "How do they know our address?"

"What? Why would I tell them?"

"I don't know. It's hard to tell with you sometimes."

"Is it?"

"Pete, do something." She does an *If you don't move now, I am going to throw something* look at him and taps her foot three times against the carpet.

Dad nods and forces himself up from the sofa. He steps into the pair of mudstruck rubber boots waiting at the door, calls Amundsen, and goes outside. I don't know what Dad expects of Amundsen. He's not a threatening mammal and will likely lick the enemy. He will roll over, offer up his belly, and make sounds like a sleepy toddler.

Mum opens the curtain partway and watches him walk down the garden path, toward a thin man with no neck and a skull-size camera lens. He's dragging Amundsen by the collar.

"Get down," Mum says. "Get away. He'll see you."

"But I want to watch."

"I don't care."

"Please."

"Put these on," she says, passing me Dad's oversize tortoiseshell reading glasses from the arm of the chair. "So he doesn't recognize you." I put the glasses on, not feeling particularly disguised, and now being partially blind. I didn't know Dad's eyes were so broken. The world has become a sequence of patches and blotches.

"What are you doing?" the Dad blur says. "I've got a dog." He points at Amundsen, who lies down in the flowerbed and rolls over, crushing a row of limp petunias.

"My petunias," Mum says.

Amundsen nibbles at soil. The journalist blur lifts his camera and another flash happens, and the Dad blur jerks forward. Both blurs fall to the ground. I take off the glasses. Dad and the journalist are wrestling like excited dogs. Dad is sitting on the journalist's face, tugging the camera from his hands. The journalist is slapping Dad around the back of his head and flailing and pedaling the air. Amundsen is watching quietly, like a child in an aquarium.

I have never seen Dad fight, and I expected it to be more impressive. I'm not disappointed, just surprised. I expected hard, swinging punches, and spit, and knuckles webbed with teeth. I think, *Maybe the reason he's sad that I'm scared isn't because he doesn't understand it.*

"Help," he shouts. "Help me." The journalist has started biting.

"Etgar, no," Mum says.

"Sorry, Mum."

I put on trainers and run out. The camera falls from the journalist's hands after I apply pressure to his wrists with my thumbs, the way the book says to. Dad climbs off and straightens himself. We face the journalist.

"That's mine," he says. I slide out the memory card and put it in my mouth.

"Here." I hand the camera back.

"Don't come again," Dad says.

"We have a dog," I say.

The journalist looks deflated and unsure. He doesn't say anything. He hangs the camera on his neck and walks quickly back to his car. Dad puts a hand on each of my shoulders. He does an *I'm not going to say anything* look, but it's calm and pleased, like a just-elected president.

Inside, Mum is walking in tight circles. "What are we going to do?" she says. "I don't know what to do."

"It's okay."

"It isn't okay. What's okay? What the fuck are we going to do?"

"Calm down," Dad says. "What we're going to do is make more tea."

"And stop swearing," I say.

"I'm sorry," Mum says. "I'm sorry to both of you. I just don't know what to do."

"I think we should do *Countdown*," I say. "Should I get paper?"

"Get paper. I don't know. Let's do *Countdown*." The phone starts to ring. Mum kneels down and unplugs it. She also unplugs the electric doorbell, turns off her computer, and, inexplicably, takes her red beret off the coat stand and places it on her head. Dad puts three teabags into three mugs and adds water.

"I'm sorry," I say. I prod Mum's knee with my right hand. It is supposed to look sympathetic, but I can't commit, and it looks random and unnatural.

"I know," Mum says.

Mum wins the first numbers round. Dad wins every letters round. He could be in dictionary corner if he wanted to. He also gets the *Countdown* conundrum within two seconds of it appearing on the screen. The *Countdown* conundrum is this:

P U L L A M A I D

"I don't like the new one," Dad says. He points at Rachel Riley. Rachel Riley smiles broadly and waves good-bye. "She's too young. What happened to Carol?"

"She moved," I say. "To *Loose Women*. She's the head one sometimes and Andrea is the head one other times."

"Do you watch a lot of *Loose Women*?"

"Pete."

"What?"

"Just don't." Mum gathers our mugs and carries them through to the kitchen. She turns on the tap. Dad flicks through channels, settling on a period drama in which three women are drinking tea on the grounds of a large country house. Mum comes back to announce that she's ready for bed. I think she may be severely disappointed in me. There's a chance that she will have another child, to raise closely and carefully, until he's a well-liked politician or a private dentist.

"Night," she says.

"Night," Dad says.

"Night," I say.

We watch the period drama in silence. Macy's sitting in my head, on the floor of a damp prison cell, about to be stabbed repeatedly with ersatz knives. She's blaming me for pulling her life apart like wet toilet paper. She's missing her children, and her belly is making dial-up sounds.

"Dad?" I say.

"Yes."

"Do you believe me that it wasn't her fault?"

"I do."

"Is there something we can do? She can't go to prison because of me. She didn't do anything. We both did something. Not something wrong."

He turns the TV off. "Tell me what happened," he says. "We can try and think of a plan."

41

I'm in bed, eating Cookies & Cream Häagen-Dazs and singing to Blink-182. It's two in the morning, and my plan is to keep eating until I go into sudden cardiac arrest and am rendered comatose. When I wake up, Macy will be free and Antarctica will be gone.

My phone rings. It's Aslam.

"This is so fucked up," he says. "Dad's going nuts. A journalist tried to interview me about you. Why didn't you answer your phone?"

"They wanted to interview you?"

"Yeah, but I said no. So they interviewed Hannah Reid."

"Who?" I push my spoon into the tub and dig out another curl of ice cream. I wonder what the fatal dose of ice cream is and if I would be able to achieve it.

"The girl we went to her party. The one with Aaron Mathews. Where he punched you."

"What did she say?"

"Wait, I'm making a cigarette." I hear muffled fumbling and the *click* of a safety lighter. He inhales. "She said she was your best friend. She said that you were totally heartbroken and hadn't stopped crying since it all started."

"She's making me sound gay."

"Really fucking gay, man. We need to do something. If you want, I can agree to the interview and tell them that you've gone around punching everyone in the face."

I think, *This is almost true.* I don't know if he's being passive-aggressive. "Punching who?"

"Just random people."

"Don't tell them that."

"Are you sure?"

"Yes."

"Fine. Will you tell me what happened? I kind of don't understand. There was just all that stuff in the papers. I'm holding one now."

"It's boring."

"Tell me."

"Okay," I say. "It's boring. I don't know. Last week, when I was being weird because of Alice, I started talking to a woman on the Internet."

I hear the *crack* of a newspaper being straightened.

"And you sent her porn of yourself."

"I did not send her porn of myself."

"That's what it says here."

"Do you want me to tell you?"

"Fine. Yes."

"We started talking, and I liked her a lot. She was like funny and stuff, and she made sense to me or something. She was fit too."

"Yeah, she looks okay. Solid seven."

"Then she told me she was going to London for a business trip, and I'd told her I lived there, so she wanted to meet. I used the money Nan left me to book a hotel and I got a train there."

"Yeah, for two nights of . . . what's debauchery?"

"I'm going to stop if you keep reading that." The word *debauchery* hangs in my head. I wonder if I'm debauched or if Macy is. I definitely don't feel debauched. I feel lost and quietly panicked.

"Fine."

"So we stayed in a hotel for two nights, and it was good, and I felt better and I didn't want to go. But I had to go because my parents were getting back. And Macy went home. But her husband was waiting for her at home with the police. She left without saying anything, left her children and stuff, and her husband found pictures of me, and our chats."

"Fuck."

"Yeah."

"Really fuck."

"Yeah."

"What's going to happen now?"

"We go to court. She could go to prison."

"For that? Why?"

"As a pedophile."

"Oh my God."

"I know."

"That can't happen."

"It's the law."

"So is 'don't smoke weed.'"

"I know."

"You got groomed by a pedo."

"Fuck off.'

I hear computer keys being tapped. I imagine his recent search history goes: Etgar Allison, Etgar Allison raped, watch *Wonder Showzen* online. "The papers are all on her side, I think. Or the comments on the *Daily Mail* site were."

"It doesn't matter."

"Guess not. What are you doing? Do you want a beer?"

"I'm eating ice cream and watching films. Really, this time. Also there might still be a photographer outside our house. Can we go on Friday?"

"Okay. I can't believe everyone cares so much."

"Me neither."

"And I can't believe you fucked a head teacher."

"She wasn't our head teacher."

"Yeah, but still."

"I know."

"I hope it gets better."

"Thanks."

"Bye, mate."

"Bye." I push my face into the near-empty ice cream tub and lick the bottom. Amundsen nudges open the door. He waits at the foot of the bed until I ask him up and he lies next to me and we climb under the duvet. I think to myself, *See you in the morning.*

42

We eat pizza for breakfast because there still isn't any other food in the house. I'm in Dad's funeral suit, and Dad's in a blue work shirt. Mum's in her dressing gown. I pull pieces of pepperoni off my pizza and sip Nesquik tea. Mum sighs, fingers her fringe, and pushes her plate away.

"You two should brush your teeth," she says.

"Okay."

Standing side by side in the bathroom mirror, foaming at our mouths, we look smaller than I thought we would look. It doesn't feel like there are butterflies in my stomach, it feels like there is vomit in it. I need to keep Macy out of prison. I can't be her dick tattoo.

Dad spits and sighs, running a hand through his hair. I mentally zoom out of the house. I keep zooming until the earth goes blue and shrinks and is gone.

43

(witness duly sworn in)

COURT: Please be seated. Would you state your full name and spell your surname?

ALLISON: Etgar Allison. A-L-L-L. Wait. Not three. Two *Ls*. Can I start again? A-L-L-I-S-O-N.

DIRECT EXAMINATION BY MR. TAYLOR

Q. Mr. Allison, how old are you?

A. Fifteen.

Q. What school do you attend?

A. St. Catherine's.

Q. Do you like it there?

A. It's okay. What? I don't know. It's fine. Six out of ten.

Q. What were you doing on the evening of April 6th?

A. Nothing. I was at home. I think I watched *Titanic*. And a program about fish. And I walked Amundsen, that's my dog. He's a mastiff, and he's sort of gray and sort of the color of sand. That doesn't matter.

Q. Had you been drinking at all?

A. I had some wine, I think, and maybe cider. Also, I think I watched cat videos on YouTube and ate Chinese food. That's for the question before. I just remembered.

Q. Did you visit a website called adultchatlife?

A. Oh, I did that. I forgot. Yes. I did.

Q. And what happened on that website?

A. People were talking about having sex with animals, specifically frogs. They were watching that video of the chimpanzee raping the frog's mouth. I made a joke about it, then Macy gave me her gmail and said we should chat.

Q. What did she say you should chat about?

A. She just said chat. She didn't say anything weird or about sex. She just wanted to talk. Just talking.

Q. And what did you talk about?

A. I don't remember. She didn't do anything. I don't know. We talked about bicycles and gardening and sewing. Just that. We talked about that.

Q. You talked about sewing?

A. Sewing buttons.

Q. How long did you talk for?

A. I don't know. A normal amount. Not a suspicious amount. Just normal. Nothing bad. She didn't do anything. No one did anything.

Q. On how many occasions did you talk?

A. I don't know.

Q. Was age ever discussed?

A. No. We never said our ages. She isn't a pedophile. She's just a woman, and that's it.

Q. Were pictures ever exchanged?

A. Yes. Dog macros mostly. And some photoshopped stills from the second and third Harry Potter films.

Q. Did you ever send the defendant pictures of yourself?

A. No.

Q. Did the defendant ever send you pictures of herself?

A. No.

Q. Were you ever asked for pictures of yourself?

A. No. She never asked for that. She never asked for anything.

Q. Where were you on the evening of April 9th?

A. I was in London. I know what question is next. Yes. I was in London with Macy. We had dinner together, then walked around, then she left and I stayed at a hotel. We talked about sewing mostly. She never showed me her vag or touched my bum. She never touched me here or here or here. We talked. That's it. Talking. People are allowed to talk to other people. That's a rule. If you don't let people talk to other people, then they become mentally ill and homicidal and do things that they should actually be in prison for.

Q. What was the name of the hotel at which you stayed?

A. She can't go to jail, she shouldn't go to jail. She never did anything. I don't remember the name of the hotel. It was biscuits color. That doesn't matter. It was stupid. The waiter.

Q. Did you stay in the hotel alone?

A. He hit her. He hit her because I don't know, and he never even talked to her and didn't touch the kids and he's a horrible piece of shit. He should be in prison, not Macy. She should be in a tree house. Let her go now. Please.

44

My eyes sting from tears, and webs of snot are leaking from my nostrils, covering my mouth. It's over. Dad comes to me, crouches a little, and picks me up the way a groom picks up a bride on their wedding day. I don't think I look capable of walking. He carries me out of the room and down the corridor. People holding stacks of paper spin to watch us pass.

The sky outside is dark with wide banks of black clouds. Heavy weather. I think about Nan and Uncle Sawicka. I try to imagine what kind of thing she would say. I think she would say the words *nonsense* and *Jesus*. Uncle Sawicka was twenty years younger, but they never got arrested because they hid in a gray corner of the planet where it perpetually rains and people spontaneously die in bathtubs. We should have done that. We should have never come out of the bed tent.

Dad lowers me onto the passenger seat. He climbs into the driver's seat, presses his head against the steering wheel, sits up straight, and starts the car.

We stop at Tesco to pick up a six-pack of Carling, then the KFC drive-through for a family-size bucket of chicken. I think we're going home, but we aren't. We follow thin roads into the hills off the motorway. Squares of yellow light from converted barns mark the way. Clusters of sheep back away from their fences. We pass several bouquets of flowers placed at a sharp bend, and I think about Amundsen's rat, and I think about the abortions, and I think about Alice's mum.

"Where are we going?"

"Wait and see."

Where we go is a wide, deep ledge, high on the hill, with parking spaces for several cars. The entire city is visible. A web of distant, orange smudges. One of them is Alice, alone in her room, talking to people who aren't me on the Internet. One of them is Aslam, sitting on a sofa with Amy's feet in his hands. One of them is Amundsen, trying to swat a moth with his paw.

Dad opens a beer and passes it to me.

"Did I do okay?" I say.

"You tried."

"I didn't seem like a victim, did I?"

He opens one for himself. "No."

"Apart from at the end."

"Maybe a little at the end."

"It's not going to work. They have the pictures and the chats, and Macy's story won't be the same as mine."

"I don't know."

"I'm scared."

"I know."

"Is it over?"

"I don't know."

I feel anxious from Dad not knowing what words to say. He can always pick words out, unless we're on the phone. I want him to talk and lay out a plan that leads us somewhere warm and without police.

"Is Mum okay?"

"She'll be okay. She just doesn't like to think of you having a penis."

"Dad."

"I'm still surprised you're not gay."

"I went out with Alice for three years."

"I know, but I always thought she'd kind of forced you to do it."

I tip the beer back until it's empty. Dad passes me another. "I don't really understand," I say. "I feel stupid."

"You're not stupid," Dad says. "But you can't always kiss who you want to kiss."

"And I'm going to be her dick tattoo."

"Wonderful."

I press my face against the window. I think about my

life randomly intersecting with other lives, tiny people bouncing off tiny people. It's too much.

Two cars pull up. "Dad," I say. "Look." We both look at the car. Two men are standing at its open window, trousers midway down, proffering their dicks. A woman with dyed scarlet hair is giving blowjobs to the dicks. One of her legs is hanging out, flapping with the beat of her head.

"What on earth?" Dad says.

"You took me dogging," I say.

"I did not take you dogging."

"I think one of them's coming over. Are you going to give him a handjob?"

"No," Dad says. "I am not." He puts the car into reverse and backs quickly out of the parking space. A tree branch snags the rear bumper. Dad swears. I laugh.

45

Me, Aslam, Sam, and Amy are celebrating nothing in the trees by the cathedral. It's full dark, and we're sitting cross-legged in a square, drinking vodka and trying not to talk about Macy. To avoid her, we have already discussed whether the weight of a T. rex would sink a cruise ship, how many words the average human knows, and whether or not the singularity is imminent.

"I think it's already happened," Aslam says. He brushes pine needles off his thighs and lights a cigarette. "Think about it. Google."

"Google isn't sentient."

"Isn't it?"

"No."

"Is *I, Robot* the singularity?"

"Yeah."

"Do you think if it happens, computers will keep us as pets?"

"No."

"Definitely yes."

I lie on my back, roll a cigarette, and light it. There aren't any stars. There are faint streetlight smudges and spotlights aimed at the cathedral walls. An ambulance somewhere moans.

"How do you tell if you have TB?"

"You don't."

"So how do people know if they have it?"

"I mean you, specifically, don't."

"I might."

A team of taller boys walks up from past the benches. I think, *We're going to be punched again.* I think, *It's okay, I'm good at it now.* I decide not to move. I decide to remain motionless on the dirt, even if they begin trampling me, even if they crack my ribs and stamp holes through my lungs.

"Hey," one of the boys says. "Is it true you got raped by that pedo teacher?"

I don't say anything.

"What if it is?" Aslam says.

"Is it?"

"No," I say.

"He had his backdoor smashed in," Aslam says. He

turns to me and does a tiny thumbs-up. "Which means bumming."

The boys laugh. "Gaylords," one says. Amy stands up, finds an empty wine bottle, and smashes it against a tree trunk.

"Go away," she says. She points the glass at them and does an *I am serious and unhinged* face.

"Jesus," one says. They mutter and leave.

"Let's go," Aslam says.

"Fine."

We leave the grounds and take Eltham Avenue up toward the bungalows. Amy sings loudly and dances, and her breath makes balls of white smoke in the air. I kick chunks of gravel along the path. I'm tired and I feel quiet.

"People are such fucking dicks," Aslam says. "People can fuck off." Amy crouches by the hood of a pristine white Mercedes, pulls off the badge, and throws it into the air. Aslam kicks it back up before it hits the ground. I pull one off the truck and toss it over the car.

We walk in the middle of the road, over a speed bump, past the infant school, stopping at each Mercedes. For a reason I don't know, Mercedes badges are the only badges to easily come off.

"Okay," Aslam says, gripping the vodka bottle like a baseball bat. "Were there really photographers?" He knocks a (Y) into the sky.

"Yeah. Dad and him wrestled."

"I like your dad."

"Me too."

"Go again." He misses the next one. "Again."

I pitch another badge, and he hits it over my head. And another. It ricochets loudly off the second-floor window of a house guarded by several garden gnomes.

"She's going to prison," Aslam says.

"I know."

"We can break her out," Amy says. "We can hide her in a laundry wagon and wheel her home."

"Yeah," Aslam says. "You can get new identities and move to Australia. Do another one." I throw another badge at him. He smacks it away. "She can get plastic surgery to change her face. Implants and shit."

"You can make money from the Internet."

"You can build a house out of driftwood."

"Or live on a boat."

"No," I say. "We can't."

Aslam flings the vodka bottle at a wall, and it shatters. I want to keep going.

I want to run through the entire neighborhood, smashing windows and lighting fires and pissing through mailboxes until the police arrive to pepper-spray me in the face and drive me away. I want to make deep scratches in the legs of the police officers. I want to head-butt them and jam my elbows into their eyes. I want to bounce myself from cell wall to cell wall until I pass out and wake up thirty hours later with a mild concussion on a day that isn't today.

46

I'm sixteen and eating stale cornflakes in the garden. Mum lifts up the teapot, fills my Forever Friends mug, and sets it back down. It's hot. I haven't been going to school. They said I could stay at home until the verdict came through, so I've watched every series of *House* and put on seven pounds.

"Eat up," Mum says.

"I am," I say. "Fat."

"You're not fat. Stop saying that. You're growing."

The weight is mostly on my cheeks and belly. Alaska is distended now and almost hanging over my belt. It's okay, though. I know what this part is. This is the part where the main character stays on the sofa, eating pizza while wearing jogging bottoms, masturbating a lot, and not answering the phone.

She plucks a green insect off her forearm. "I love you."

"I know."

Eventually, the next part will begin. Something will happen that causes staccato violin music to start playing, and I will lace up my trainers, drink a Gatorade, and run, stiffly at first, then quickly and with wild arms.

The sunroom doors open and Dad appears. He is doing an *I don't want to show what's in my head* face. He walks until he is standing behind me, puts his hands on my shoulders, and squeezes.

"Massage," I say. He starts to press his thumbs into the space between my shoulder blades. "Happy ending," I say. Dad reaches over me, toward my crotch, and I jump and fall onto the patio.

"Pete," Mum says.

"Yeah," I say. "Jesus, Pete." His hands hook under my armpits and lift me up and lower me back into the chair. I take a sip of tea. Dad fits his left fingers through his right fingers.

"No jail," he says. "They want her to go to a psychiatric hospital, and she won't be allowed to work with children again."

Nothing happens. Amundsen noses open the door and pads out to us. I prop my feet up on his back. I close my eyes. I think I might start to dissolve soon.

Acknowledgments

I forgot to do acknowledgments last time, and I'm sorry. Hi, everyone. Thank you for being nice to me: Mum, Clive, Beth. Nan, Grampy. Sam, Lisa. Buse, Millie. Crispin, Dan. Jon. Jan, Diana, Alice, Lino. Barcelona. Team Pop Serial. Francis, Jamie, Canongate. Ron, Judith, Regan Arts. You are all 10/10s.

BEN BROOKS

is the author of five previous
books including *Grow Up* (in
development for television in
the UK), *Fences*, and *An Island
of Fifty*. His work has been
longlisted for the Dylan Thomas
Prize, nominated for a Pushcart
Prize, and published in the
Dzanc Best of the Web anthology.
He lives in Gloucestershire,
England and was born in 1992.